FACE OF MADNESS

EUROPEAN VOYAGE COZY MYSTERY SERIES

MURDER (AND BAKLAVA) (Book #1) √

DEATH (AND APPLE STRUDEL) (Book #2)

CRIME (AND LAGER) (Book #3)

ADELE SHARP MYSTERY SERIES

LEFT TO DIE (Book #1)

LEFT TO RUN (Book #2)

LEFT TO HIDE (Book #3)

LEFT TO KILL (Book #4)

LEFT TO MURDER (Book #5)

LEFT TO ENVY (Book #6)

LEFT TO LAPSE (Book #7)

THE AU PAIR SERIES

ALMOST GONE (Book#1)

ALMOST LOST (Book #2)

ALMOST DEAD (Book #3)

ZOE PRIME MYSTERY SERIES

FACE OF DEATH (Book#1) √

FACE OF MURDER (Book #2) √

FACE OF FEAR (Book #3) √

FACE OF MADNESS (Book #4) √

FACE OF FURY (Book #5) √

FACE OF DARKNESS (Book #6) √

A JESSIE HUNT PSYCHOLOGICAL SUSPENSE SERIES

THE PERFECT WIFE (Book #1)
THE PERFECT BLOCK (Book #2)
THE PERFECT HOUSE (Book #3)
THE PERFECT SMILE (Book #4)
THE PERFECT LIE (Book #5)
THE PERFECT LOOK (Book #6)
THE PERFECT AFFAIR (Book #7)
THE PERFECT ALIBI (Book #8)
THE PERFECT NEIGHBOR (Book #9)
THE PERFECT DISGUISE (Book #10)
THE PERFECT SECRET (Book #11)

CHLOE FINE PSYCHOLOGICAL SUSPENSE SERIES

NEXT DOOR (Book #1)
A NEIGHBOR'S LIE (Book #2)
CUL DE SAC (Book #3)
SILENT NEIGHBOR (Book #4)
HOMECOMING (Book #5)
TINTED WINDOWS (Book #6)

KATE WISE MYSTERY SERIES

IF SHE KNEW (Book #1) ✓
IF SHE SAW (Book #2)
IF SHE RAN (Book #3)
IF SHE HID (Book #4)
IF SHE FLED (Book #5)
IF SHE FEARED (Book #6)
IF SHE HEARD (Book #7)

THE MAKING OF RILEY PAIGE SERIES

WATCHING (Book #1)
WAITING (Book #2)
LURING (Book #3)
TAKING (Book #4)

STALKING (Book #5)
KILLING (Book #6)

RILEY PAIGE MYSTERY SERIES

ONCE GONE (Book #1)
ONCE TAKEN (Book #2)
ONCE CRAVED (Book #3)
ONCE LURED (Book #4)
ONCE HUNTED (Book #5)
ONCE PINED (Book #6)
ONCE FORSAKEN (Book #7)
ONCE COLD (Book #8)
ONCE STALKED (Book #9)
ONCE LOST (Book #10)
ONCE BURIED (Book #11)
ONCE BOUND (Book #12)
ONCE TRAPPED (Book #13)
ONCE DORMANT (Book #14)
ONCE SHUNNED (Book #15)
ONCE MISSED (Book #16)
ONCE CHOSEN (Book #17)

MACKENZIE WHITE MYSTERY SERIES

BEFORE HE KILLS (Book #1)
BEFORE HE SEES (Book #2)
BEFORE HE COVETS (Book #3)
BEFORE HE TAKES (Book #4)
BEFORE HE NEEDS (Book #5)
BEFORE HE FEELS (Book #6)
BEFORE HE SINS (Book #7)
BEFORE HE HUNTS (Book #8)
BEFORE HE PREYS (Book #9)
BEFORE HE LONGS (Book #10)
BEFORE HE LAPSES (Book #11)
BEFORE HE ENVIES (Book #12)

BEFORE HE STALKS (Book #13)
BEFORE HE HARMS (Book #14)

AVERY BLACK MYSTERY SERIES
CAUSE TO KILL (Book #1)
CAUSE TO RUN (Book #2)
CAUSE TO HIDE (Book #3)
CAUSE TO FEAR (Book #4)
CAUSE TO SAVE (Book #5)
CAUSE TO DREAD (Book #6)

KERI LOCKE MYSTERY SERIES
A TRACE OF DEATH (Book #1) ✓
A TRACE OF MUDER (Book #2) ✓
A TRACE OF VICE (Book #3) ✓
A TRACE OF CRIME (Book #4) ✓
A TRACE OF HOPE (Book #5) ✓

FACE OF MADNESS

(A Zoe Prime Mystery—Book 4)

BLAKE PIERCE

BLAKE PIERCE

Blake Pierce is the USA Today bestselling author of the RILEY PAGE mystery series, which includes seventeen books. Blake Pierce is also the author of the MACKENZIE WHITE mystery series, comprising fourteen books; of the AVERY BLACK mystery series, comprising six books; of the KERI LOCKE mystery series, comprising five books; of the MAKING OF RILEY PAIGE mystery series, comprising six books; of the KATE WISE mystery series, comprising seven books; of the CHLOE FINE psychological suspense mystery, comprising six books; of the JESSE HUNT psychological suspense thriller series, comprising seven books (and counting); of the AU PAIR psychological suspense thriller series, comprising two books (and counting); of the ZOE PRIME mystery series, comprising five books (and counting); of the new ADELE SHARP mystery series; and of the new EUROPEAN VOYAGE cozy mystery series.

ONCE GONE (a Riley Paige Mystery—Book #1), BEFORE HE KILLS (A Mackenzie White Mystery—Book I), CAUSE TO KILL (An Avery Black Mystery—Book I), A TRACE OF DEATH (A Keri Locke Mystery—Book I), WATCHING (The Making of Riley Paige—Book I), NEXT DOOR (A Chloe Fine Psychological Suspense Mystery—Book I), THE PERFECT WIFE (A Jessie Hunt Psychological Suspense Thriller—Book One), and IF SHE KNEW (A Kate Wise Mystery—Book I) are each available as a free download on Amazon!

An avid reader and lifelong fan of the mystery and thriller genres, Blake loves to hear from you, so please feel free to visit www.blakepierceauthor.com to learn more and stay in touch.

TABLE OF CONTENTS

CHAPTER ONE

Zoe let her eyes drift to the familiar, well-worn arm of the chair. The leather was cracked in different directions from the grip and trace of many hands and fingers, a fact that used to make her mind go into overdrive, making calculations and tracking patterns. Her special ability, the power to see the numbers in everything around her, had so often been a hindrance rather than a help. But now, looking at the leather, she was able to see only a chair and not an equation.

She looked away, still focused on the moment and the question at hand. "I am looking forward to tonight," she said, smiling at Dr. Lauren Monk, her therapist. The woman had changed her hair recently, cutting in a dark fringe above her dark eyes, and it suited her. She looked five years younger.

"Tell me about your plans," Dr. Monk said. Her head rested at a tilt on one of her hands, and she was studying Zoe closely. Zoe couldn't help but notice that her notebook had remained closed for the duration of the session, and the pen dangled loosely in her hand.

"I am doing something I have never done before," Zoe said, feeling the flush of excitement color her cheeks slightly. "A double date. John and I, along with Shelley and her husband."

"You feel that you'll be able to thrive in this situation?"

"Yes." Zoe nodded her head, knowing it was the truth. Not only because of Dr. Monk's help, but also because she had come to trust John, after dating him for months. Shelley, her partner at work, had also proven time and again that she could support Zoe whenever she needed it. "The exercises you gave me have been keeping the numbers down. I don't think I will be overwhelmed. Not this time."

Dr. Monk's lips quirked upward briefly as Zoe spoke, as if she'd heard something that made her extremely happy. She had a beauty mark half an inch above the right edge of her mouth, and it jumped up too. With a flourish, she set her notebook aside firmly on the table, setting the pen on top of it neatly. "Zoe, I'm going to say something, and please don't take it the wrong way," she said. Her expression was all captured mirth, as if she didn't want to reveal how happy she was. "I think it's time we stop seeing one another."

Zoe raised an eyebrow. "You think I should see a different therapist?"

Dr. Monk laughed. "No, Zoe. What did I say about taking it the wrong way? I don't think you need to see a therapist at all."

"We are ... done?"

Dr. Monk nodded in confirmation. "You don't need me anymore."

Zoe cast her eyes around the room that Dr. Monk employed for her therapy sessions: the certificates framed in black wood on the wall, the bookshelves full of psychology books, the potted plant in the corner. A sudden pang of nostalgia hit her, something that she didn't often feel as an FBI agent—always in one place only for long enough to not yet be used to it before the case was done. It was the sensation of leaving a place for the last time. "What if I start to lose control again?"

Dr. Monk leaned forward, placing her hand on top of Zoe's where it rested on the arm of the chair. "If you ever need me again, all you have to do is pick up the phone and make an appointment. You'll always be on my patient list. But this is our last regular session."

Zoe nodded, letting it wash over her. She was done with therapy. No longer needed it. It had been a long series of months sitting in this chair, and she had put a lot of work into trying to change. Hearing that she had at last been victorious was really only confirmation. She knew, as she looked inside herself, that she had conquered the worst parts of her mind, tamed them and trained them.

She cast her eyes around the room again, a little self-test. The numbers were still there, whenever she wanted them to be. She could know at a glance that there was one fewer book on the shelves—perhaps Dr. Monk had taken it down to read or given it to someone for study. She knew the bookshelves were seven feet tall, and that Dr. Monk probably had to stand on something to reach the volumes at the very top.

But when she looked again, concentrating this time on staying calm, she just saw a bookcase filled with books. Like everyone else did.

She felt a curve lifting her lips, without her permission. A real, natural smile, something that came to her rarely. She felt stronger than she ever had. Better. More ready, for whatever might be coming her way.

"Thank you, Dr. Monk," she said, getting to her feet and holding out her hand.

The doctor shook it, gripping her tighter for a moment with a watery smile of pride, and then escorted her to the door.

"Please don't take this the wrong way," Zoe said, playfully, as she turned on the threshold. "But I hope I do not have to see you for a long time."

Dr. Monk answered her with a glittering smile. "I feel the same," she said, closing the door on her with a laugh.

Zoe squared her shoulders. Personal victories required celebration. It was just as well, then, that she had somewhere special to be.

Another door opened at Zoe's knock, several hours later and in a different part of town. Despite Dr. Monk's words of support, she felt jittery now and nervous, her hands seemingly unable to stay still. She turned the handle of her bag over between her fingers, twisting the thin strap one way and then another.

Dr. Francesca Applewhite's still-slim frame was wrapped in a comfortable robe, and her gray-streaked dark hair bounced up and then down in its neat bob as she took Zoe in from head to foot. "Zoe," she said, clearly trying to choose her words carefully. "I wasn't expecting you. You look lovely. But, ah ... what happened to your eyes?"

Zoe almost crumpled, her gaze hitting the floor. She knew she had failed. "I need your help," she said miserably.

Dr. Applewhite moved forward immediately, taking her by the elbow. "All right, my dear. Come in, come in."

Zoe followed her beloved mentor into her comfortable home. The corridor was lined with framed achievements: both Dr. Applewhite and her husband were accomplished, and though they had never had children, the certificates and awards spoke of academic careers and lives lived in the service of research.

"I have never done it before," Zoe whined, hating even as she did so the way her voice sounded so defeated and high-pitched. "I thought it would be easy. I watched YouTube tutorials to see how to do it but…"

Dr. Applewhite paused, turning to place a hand between Zoe's shoulder blades as she guided her along. "Don't worry. It's an easy fix. We'll get you sorted out. Big night tonight, is it?"

"Date night," Zoe said, already feeling better at the prospect of getting help from the one person who had always been there for her when needed.

Although perhaps that wasn't fair. She had known Shelley only for a relatively short time, compared to Dr. Applewhite, but she had never let Zoe down either. Even at the times when Zoe had been angry at her for presumed slights, she had always later come to see that Shelley had made the right choice. A few months ago, when they had worked together to bring down a serial killer targeting people with Holocaust memorial tattoos, Shelley had put all of her faith in Zoe to focus their resources on finding the killer when they already had a different suspect in custody. It had worked, and they were more in synergy now than ever, working instinctively to solve their cases and trusting one another implicitly.

Come to think of it, John, too, had never let her down. He was always the one who showed up, often first, often waiting for her. He had never become frustrated or angry when Zoe needed to cancel a date because she was out on a case in another part of the country, even when it came up last minute.

Somehow, gradually and without realizing it, Zoe had managed to surround herself with the kind of people on whom she could depend.

"All right, sit on the edge of the bath," Dr. Applewhite said, ushering Zoe into a white, marble-lined bathroom and bustling over to a cabinet. It turned out to be full of various makeup and skincare products. She drew out a bottle of something which she tilted against a cotton pad, a swift and practiced motion.

"What are you going to do?" Zoe asked, eyeing the bottle with alarm. All of this was beyond her normal understanding. She had never been the kind of woman who tried to look pretty. She kept her brown hair cropped short for convenience, and everything was about the job. Practicality. Comfortable, plain clothes that were easy to move in, flat shoes for running. A clean face, because she had to be on the road at the drop of a hat, and rain could fling mascara into your eyes just when you were on the heels of a suspect. The field of beauty was alien to her, save for a few experiments in college that had never gone well.

"Tilt your head back, and close your eyes," Dr. Applewhite said. Without thinking, Zoe obeyed her blindly. Dr. Applewhite was a full four inches shorter than her, and didn't have far down to lean now that Zoe was on the edge of the bath. "I'm going to take off these panda eyes you've given yourself and start again. Let me guess—you couldn't get them even, so you kept adding a bit more to each side to try and make them equal?"

Zoe nodded, then froze as the feel of the cotton wool pad soaked in something wet swept across her closed eyelid. "I have the eyeliner with me," she said. "I am sorry for coming over like this. I didn't know who else to ask for help."

"Don't worry," Dr. Applewhite said, her voice a little distant with concentration. "I'm always here for you, Zoe. You know that. Now, give me the eyeliner."

Zoe fumbled in her bag to hand it over, then obediently closed her eyes again. Dr. Applewhite's firm and steady hand brushed over each of her eyelids again, one by one, a light pressure that flicked out a well-practiced line.

"There," Dr. Applewhite said, sounding quietly pleased with herself. "Take a look."

Zoe opened her eyes, blinking in the bright lights of the bathroom while her eyes readjusted. She stood and headed to the bathroom mirror, and caught her breath.

Dr. Applewhite had drawn elegant, thin lines with the black paint, sweeping along the curve of her eyelid and then flicking out just a tiny tail at the edges. The liner drew out the darkness in her brown eyes, contrasted it against the lighter flecks of color in her irises. Zoe had never seen herself like this before. She looked exotic. Feminine.

"Happy?" Dr. Applewhite asked. "I can do something else if you want."

Zoe nodded, biting her lip. "Happy," she said.

"Tonight must be special," Dr. Applewhite said, sitting down on the closed lid of the toilet.

Zoe resumed her position on the side of the bath, perching there like a teenager. "I am going on a double date with John, Shelley, and her husband," she explained. "I wanted to make an effort."

"Well, you look beautiful," Dr. Applewhite said, gesturing to the deep crimson dress Zoe had picked out. "I've never seen you wear something like this."

Zoe looked down. She had, at first, felt uncomfortable with the way the dress dipped low across her cleavage, the way it clung to her hips and the slit in the fabric that ran to her lower thigh. She had been even more uncomfortable in the shoes, though the heel was barely more than an inch high. It was all new to her. "I wanted to show him that I can be . . ." She sought the word. "Womanly."

Dr. Applewhite leaned over and grasped Zoe's hand in hers. "He knows that already. John has stuck with you this long. You don't have to change for him."

"I know." Zoe hesitated, trying to sum up the feeling. "It is more that . . . I want to."

Dr. Applewhite smiled, a deep and genuine smile that seemed to stem from her eyes and reach her lips second. "Things are getting serious with him."

It wasn't a question, but Zoe felt compelled to answer it anyway. "Maybe. Tonight . . ." Zoe took a deep breath. This was the thing that was really making her jittery with nerves, the thing that had pushed her to make more of an effort with her appearance. "Tonight, I want to talk with him. Really talk. About our future, and where the relationship is going."

Dr. Applewhite's eyes, lined as they were with the wrinkles of a life of frequent smiles, were shining with moisture. Everyone seemed to be like that around her lately. Zoe wondered if flu season was getting an early start. "What do you hope for him to say?"

Zoe looked down at her bitten fingernails. She had attempted to put on some nail varnish that morning, but it had not gone well. In the end, she had scrubbed it all away and resolved to focus on her face. "I do not know," she admitted. "Things have been going well between us, but sooner or later they have to go forward or stop. I am . . ."

Dr. Applewhite spoke up, completing the sentence for her. "Afraid?"

Zoe inclined her head. "A little."

"And what about the numbers?" Dr. Applewhite asked, cutting right to the heart of the matter as she always did. "Does he know yet?"

"No," Zoe sighed. The number of people who knew about her secret, her ability to see the numbers in everything, she could count on one hand. Shelley,

Dr. Monk, Dr. Applewhite, and her physician. Those who had to know, and those who had worked it out for themselves.

"Do you think you might tell him?" Dr. Applewhite prompted, gently.

Zoe turned her hands over, studied the lines on her palms. Some people, she knew, believed that you could read a fortune there in the length and angle of the lines. It was the kind of thinking that might have been addictive for her, if she had believed any of it. "Perhaps," she said, tracing the line that she knew was thought to be connected to love. "Depending on tonight."

Dr. Applewhite stood abruptly, starting to bustle around. She hid her face from Zoe to busy herself in the bathroom cabinet. "I hope it goes well," she said, her voice strangely strained. "I really do."

"Thank you," Zoe said. "I mean, for everything."

To her surprise, Dr. Applewhite spun around then and swept her into an embrace, a light clutch and squeeze around her shoulders. When she released her, Dr. Applewhite was patting at her eyes, turning Zoe toward the door with a gentle push. "I don't know why you're wasting time with an old woman like me," she said. "You've got a big date to get to. Go on, now. Go have fun."

Privately, Zoe wondered if it was going to be fun after all. There was a lot riding on the outcome of her conversation with John, and this was also a chance to make a better impression on Shelley's husband than she had the last time she met.

As she stepped out into the street and headed for her car, Zoe felt the weight of pressure settling on her shoulders. It joined the nerves thrumming through her, until she almost thought she might drive straight home.

But, sitting in the driver's seat, she squared her shoulders one more time and faced dead ahead. She was going to get this done, even if it was going to be the death of her.

It was too important to chicken out now.

CHAPTER TWO

Lorna shaded her eyes against the late August sun, looking out over the view from the ridge. Out across the horizon rose wind turbines, white and soaring over green fields, outcrops of shrubs, sunken dips, and water reflecting blue sky. Soon, all of the greenery would start to turn orange or brown, but for now it was still bright and full of life. A palette of greens and blues and whites. Perfect for a day's hike.

Lorna turned and looked back the way she had come, at the buildings of the town behind her. She was close enough still that from this distance she could recognize some of them: a church, a community center, the library beside an open strip of land that was one of the parks. Her home. She had lived in this small Nebraska town her whole life, but with plenty of hiking trails around and all the amenities one could want, she had never thought of going elsewhere.

She turned her eyes back to the trail ahead and began to walk again. Mentally, she was plotting her course for the rest of the day: down across this ridge and over the next, past the base of the first turbine—always comically larger than she expected—and on. She would stop when she reached a favorite spot of hers, a lake that, if you squinted, was almost shaped like a heart. Rest there a while, then turn on a circular route back toward town and her car before heading home in time for dinner.

She wondered about stopping by the store on the way home, getting something pre-made so she wouldn't have to cook. It might be nice. A reward for the day's exertion.

There was a spring in her step as she trod along the well-loved trail, following in the footsteps of so many others as well as her own ghost, leading the way before her on the hundreds of trips she must have taken out here. She was lucky, living so close to a set of trails that offered beauty and variety. She didn't have to drive out to the middle of nowhere like they did in other places. The safety of home was always just at her back.

Lorna took a deep breath of the fresh air as she crested another ridge, flexing her shoulders and feeling the heat of the sun on them. With her baseball cap shading her head and face, she enjoyed the heat. Her bare arms, lathered with sunscreen before she had set off, were free to catch the breeze, keeping her body temperature comfortable. It was almost the perfect day for it. In her mind's eye she sketched the view, a familiar sight on all sides that she could draw from memory.

She looked down and nearly stumbled, catching herself before she walked right into another traveler sitting down on the rocky trail just below the summit of the ridge. It was a man, nursing his ankle with a discarded hiking boot by his hand.

"Oh!" she exclaimed, finding her feet again. "God, I didn't see you. Sorry—I nearly fell right over you!"

He gave a short laugh, tilting his head back to look at her from under the brim of his own cap. "Oh, wow, no, I'm sorry—that's my fault. I should know better than to sit right in a blind spot."

"Are you all right?" Lorna asked. Now that he had his head back, she could see he was quite attractive. Classical looks—a strong nose, defined cheekbones, a masculine jaw almost like three straight lines on a page. He was young, too, probably in his early thirties. Her heart fluttered a little in her chest. Almost without knowing she was doing it, she straightened her back, pushing her chest out, internally wishing she had worn more than the barest touch of makeup.

"Oh, yeah," he said, dismissively, waving a hand as he looked down at his ankle again. "Stupid, really. Just a little sprain, I think."

"What happened?" Lorna asked. Her hands flexed on the straps of her backpack, and she dropped them down by her sides.

He pointed to a rock, not far from the summit of the ridge. "Turned my ankle coming down off the ridge on that rock, there. I was looking at the view instead of where I was walking. Rookie mistake, right?"

Lorna smiled. "Right. Stop and watch the view, then watch the ground when you're walking."

"I know, I know," he said, shrugging helplessly. "I guess that teaches me to try hiking somewhere new."

"Do you need me to call someone?" Lorna asked. Her hands flew to her pocket, where her cell phone waited in case of emergency. "Or help you up?"

"I'll be all right," he said, reaching for his boot and starting to put it back on. "Got to get back on the horse. It'll feel better once I walk it off, I think."

"Are you sure?" Lorna hesitated, worriedly watching him. Her friends said she had a tendency to be a mother hen. She couldn't help it. Seeing someone in need, and not helping, made her feel anxious.

"Yeah, yeah," he said, tying up his laces. "Honestly. I feel so stupid. Just my luck that it would be a pretty woman who finds me regretting a stupid mistake, huh?"

Lorna's cheeks heated a little at his words. He had called her pretty, but thrown it in as if it were nothing, not even looking at her as he used his own steam to get tentatively to his feet. Like it was a clear fact that needed no further discussion or an exchange of looks, because it was obvious to both of them.

She stepped back a little to give him room, one hand flying unconsciously out to hover near him in case he needed support. He hopped and shuffled a little as he stood, testing his weight on the ankle, before he eased into a more or less even distribution on both feet. An easy stance, comfortable and practiced, despite the pain.

"Are you sure you're good?" Lorna asked. She watched him with doubt, half-expecting him to stumble and drop to the floor again.

He tested the foot some more, gradually shifting until most of his weight was on it. "Seems like it," he said, flashing her a grin. "I'm not going to risk it, though. I'll just head back to my car and get on home."

"Let me walk with you," Lorna offered immediately, both because it was the right thing to do and because, secretly, she wanted to spend some more time with this handsome stranger. Maybe, if he was local, they could end up exchanging numbers and plan to go hiking together someday soon.

"I don't want to put you out," he said, just as quickly. "I'm sure you had your own plans, and I'm just getting in the way. You're only just starting your hike, right?"

Her breath caught in her throat for a moment. "How did you know that?"

He gestured out the way she had come. "You came from the direction of the parking lot at the foot of the trail. Same as me."

She nodded, smiling at her own paranoia. "Of course," she said. "Well, I don't mind. I wouldn't feel right, leaving you to walk back on your own. If I came across you sitting on the ground on the way back because you didn't make it, I'd feel pretty bad."

His lips, which were bow-shaped with a fullness that made them entirely kissable, curved into a smile. "All right," he said. "I wouldn't want to make you feel bad. I guess, let's go."

They turned together and began to walk back in the direction of their cars. Overhead, a single white cloud scudded across the blue sky, driven by the gentle breeze. "It's a nice day for it," Lorna said.

"Sure is," he laughed. "That's why I thought I'd better get out here while I have the chance. Not every day that good weather coincides with a day off work."

"I'm kind of surprised," Lorna said, walking along the side of the path so that he could take the most even part of the ground. "I thought there would be a lot of folks out today. Trail's quiet."

"Most people are at home, I guess," he said, indicating the town in the distance. From a few of the nearer points, it was possible to make out thin trails of black smoke. "Cooking up a storm on the grill."

Lorna nodded, shading her eyes to look over toward the town. "You're right," she said. "I didn't even think of that." She didn't add the reason why: that she was single, of course, and didn't have a whole lot of family to spend time with. Hiking was her thing all over: quiet, solitude, time to think.

Mind you, sharing it with someone else was turning out not to be so bad, after all.

"Personally, I'd rather be out on the trails any day," he said. When she looked back at him, lagging just behind her steps, he smiled with a twinkle in his eye. "I've got no girl to go home to, so I spend as much time as I can out in the open air. I live a couple of towns over. That's why I'm not usually around here."

"Oh, yeah?" Lorna asked, her mind working. He was single, local, and undeniably attractive. This was shaping up to be quite the opportune meeting. She just wondered how she would broach the subject. Maybe she should wait for him to bring it up first, or casually mention something about showing him the trails if he wanted to try them again.

"Hey, maybe you could show me around here sometime," he said, making her heart quicken. "Would that be all right? I mean, once my ankle's strong again."

"Sure," she said. She didn't dare look around at him, in case he saw the pink color high in her cheeks. "I'd like that."

"I'm sure glad we met up today, Lorna," he said, and she wholeheartedly agreed with the sentiment.

Then missed a step, realizing that he had said her name.

When had she told him her name?

She opened her mouth to ask if they'd met somewhere before, because how else could he know who she was? But even as she did so and began to turn to face him, something solid connected with the back of her head, right in a painful spot that seemed to rock her brain against her skull.

Lorna opened her eyes to find that she was on the ground, even though she had only blinked. There was a sharp pain ricocheting through her head, and as she groggily reached up to check for blood, she caught sight of him. Standing over her now, all trace of the favored ankle now gone. He was straight and tall, his posture strong, unyielding. There was a leather blackjack hanging from his left hand, which she dimly understood must have been the source of the pain in her head.

"Wha...?" she tried to ask. She was sleepy, despite the pain, and everything seemed as though it was moving through treacle.

"Don't move," he told her. His voice was flat and hard now, like a piece of slate.

She didn't exactly intend to obey him, but on the other hand there was not much else that she could do. Lorna stopped groping through her own hair to find the source of the pain and attempted instead to roll over, a slow process that made her gasp and pause while her brain rocked and pounded.

He came back into her field of view from behind a clump of low bushes. Something else was in his hand now. It was long and glinted in the sun, the gleam of silver. Dimly, trying to fight a wave of nausea as she turned over, Lorna recognized what it must be: a sword of some kind, with a slight curve toward the end of the blade.

"I said," he growled, coming closer and standing over her, blocking out the sun, "don't move."

Lorna looked up. The sun shot rays out from behind his head, leaving his face in black shadow. He raised the machete up, over his head, and moved his feet slightly, like he was finding the right posture. Lorna put one curled fist forward to crawl away, trying to move, to do anything that would help her escape.

There was a swishing sound as the machete came down toward her, and Lorna closed her eyes so that she wouldn't have to see.

CHAPTER THREE

This is all fine, Zoe reminded herself, looking between Shelley's laughing face and John's, pasting a smile on her own to mimic them. Across from her, Harry—Shelley's husband—was smoothing down his tie, quietly pleased with himself at a joke well told. It was a gesture so like one of John's that Zoe had to stop herself from doing a double-take. What was it about ties that begged to be smoothed down?

"This was a great idea, Shelley," John said, raising his glass of wine toward her before taking a sip. He'd picked out yet another blue striped shirt for the dinner date. Zoe had been keeping track of how many he owned, and it seemed to be quite a lot.

"It was," Harry agreed. "It's nice to get to know your colleagues a bit better." He offered a gentle smile to Zoe, as if to let her know that everything was forgiven. Together with his messy brown hair, which always seemed kind of softly wild, it gave him a somewhat genial look.

For her part, Zoe flushed a little, though she returned the smile. Last time she had been invited to have dinner with Harry and Shelley, she had run out of the house in a panic, feeling the weight of Shelley's perfect life crushing down on her.

But that had been before. Before Dr. Monk had helped her, before she had gained control over the numbers that had colored every moment of her life until then. Before she could ever imagine sitting in a busy restaurant with three other people, with crisscrossing and overlapping conversations, and being able to keep up with it all.

"Your main courses," the waiter announced, appearing behind Zoe with four plates balanced along his arm and in his hand. There was a general murmur of approval around the table, everyone drawing their hands and elbows back, making way.

Zoe looked down at her plate as it was placed before her, her eyes flicking across the side salad. Counting five leaves of iceberg lettuce, three of romaine, two cherry tomatoes, one quarter of a sliced bell pepper—

She closed her eyes briefly, finding her way to a tranquil beach island with nothing around but the gentle lapping of waves. Under the table, John's hand found hers and squeezed. Her eyes flew open to fix him with a smile, and she breathed again, putting the numbers back into the background where they belonged. He didn't even know her secret, and yet he still seemed to instinctively know when she needed comfort.

"It looks delicious," Zoe said, sneaking a glance at the others' plates and finding the same.

There were noises of agreement around the table, and clattering as each of them picked up their cutlery and started to dig in. The arrival of the food was both welcome and unwelcome. It provided an excuse not to have to keep up with constant conversation, but also left the table shrouded in silence, something that always made Zoe uncomfortable.

Well, truth be told, she was most comfortable of all when there was silence. But she knew the social expectations of the others, the pressure that would demand the silence to be filled. She looked up anxiously and caught John's eye, and he grinned at her around his fork. She reached for her glass of wine and took a sip, reassured that this was how things were supposed to be.

The main course passed smoothly enough, with snatches of conversation here and there that receded again into the general enjoyment of food, seemingly without awkwardness. Zoe remained alert, her head darting up and around the table regularly, watching out for social cues that she might otherwise miss. It kept her present, kept the numbers off her mind. She was able to take part, instead of sitting on the sidelines and feeling overwhelmed like she used to.

"Now, John, you're a lawyer, isn't that right?" Harry asked, scooping his last bite of fish into his mouth.

John nodded, hurriedly finishing a mouthful before speaking. "I'm in property law. Estate inheritance, real estate deals, boundary disputes—that kind of thing."

"Must keep you pretty busy," Harry commented. Zoe had never understood this kind of small talk, and she still didn't now. Why didn't Harry ask what he really wanted to know? Instead, they all had to shroud their meaning in polite, vague questions to try to fish for it. Zoe was glad she was on friendly enough terms with at least John and Shelley to not be expected to resort to that.

"Busy enough," John replied, the hint of a smile around his lips. He set down his fork momentarily to brush a hand over his close-cropped brown hair, a habitual gesture. Zoe eyed the flex of the muscles in his arm and shoulder under his shirt and told herself to concentrate. "I've just finished working on a real doozy of a case. Two brothers, fighting over their late father's estate. The two of them were just about willing to crucify one another over a few extra yards. Couldn't seem to accept things the way the old man wanted them."

Shelley shook her head ruefully. "I don't know how people can get so heartless," she said. "Family is everything. It's not right, going up against one another like that."

"Family is not everything to everyone," Zoe said quietly. "Some people do not cherish blood."

Shelley gave her a startled and apologetic look. She had no doubt forgotten, in the moment, Zoe's troubled relationship—or lack thereof—with her own mother. "You're right," she said. "Of course. I suppose I just find it hard to imagine going up against my own family like that."

"That's because you've got a big heart," Harry said, squeezing his wife's hand on the table. They looked at one another lovingly for a moment, and Zoe found her eyes drawn away—from what felt like a private look—toward John, who was watching her with a curious smile on his face.

"Do we feel like dessert?" John asked, tidying his knife and fork to sit flat on his empty plate.

Harry and Shelley exchanged something meaningful in their eyes before nodding in unison. "Why not?" Harry said. "I'll try and get someone's attention to bring over the menus."

"Good," Shelley replied, putting her napkin up on the table beside her plate. "While you do that, Zoe and I will go to the ladies' room."

Zoe blinked. "I don't need to use the ladies' room," she said, baffled that Shelley would have announced it for her.

Shelley gave her a coy look, bending down slightly from where she stood to murmur in Zoe's ear. "You don't have to need to. I need to. You're coming with me."

"Why?" Zoe asked, blinking again.

"For company," Shelley said. Then, with an impatient gesture and a little gasp of frustration: "To gossip about our menfolk where they can't hear us. Come on."

Zoe still wasn't quite sure she understood, but she got up anyway, following her partner with a somewhat hesitant step. Not because she was indecisive about following her—she trusted Shelley enough to do what she wanted—but because she had forgotten she was wearing heels until she stood up, and the alien sensation at the end of her legs was making her off-balance. Shelley, meanwhile, walked with confidence in her stilettos, her curvy hips swaying from side to side with grace.

"Is that why women always go to the bathroom together?" Zoe asked, as they pushed open the door of the room to find a few other women already in there, washing their hands and peering at themselves in the mirrors over the sinks.

"Yes," Shelley said, laughing. "And for comfort and companionship. Because it's nice. And because men hunt in packs, so why shouldn't we?"

Zoe had to admit, Shelley had a point. She hid a smile as she stood, leaning against the unoccupied, folded-away changing table—the most out-of-the-way she could be in the small space. She caught sight of herself in a floor-length mirror near the door, not recognizing herself for a moment. Dr. Applewhite's ministrations had pulled attention to her eyes, and her figure—that she often thought of as boyish, with no hips or chest to speak of—had been given artificial swoops and curves by the cut of the dress. Even her hair in its pixie cut somehow looked softer and more feminine tonight, balanced out by red-stoned drop earrings that felt heavy and unfamiliar.

One by one, the other women finished preening themselves and walked back out into the restaurant, so that when Shelley emerged from her cubicle the two of them were alone.

Shelley started washing her hands, looking up at Zoe in a way that made her come closer for the conversation that was obviously wanted. "You're doing really well," she said, turning off the faucet.

"I am?"

Shelley looked at her sideways as she moved to dry her hands on loose paper towels. "You know you are. But still, it bears saying. I'm proud of you. When we first partnered up, I never thought you'd be able to do something like this."

Zoe had to admit she was right. "I never thought that I would want to, let alone be able to."

"Well, then I'm glad we could change your mind on that," Shelley said, finishing off with the towels and coming to stand in front of her. "You look beautiful, Zoe. I love this new look on you."

Zoe smiled, feeling an unfamiliar flush rise to her cheeks. "It took some practice," she said, stopping just short of admitting that it had also taken help. She took Shelley in at a glance: always perfectly made up and elegant, today was no exception. Her blonde hair was in a slightly fancier bun than normal, with twists and coils that looked complicated, and the pale shade of pink on her eyelids matched the fabric of her demure yet figure-hugging dress. She looked, well, like she always did: just right for the occasion.

"The practice paid off," Shelley said, picking up her purse from where she had set it down beside the sink.

Zoe, sensing that the appropriate moment for returning the compliment had passed, panicked for a second before deciding to throw it out anyway. "You look really nice, too."

Shelley rewarded her with a beam, giving her own reflection a glance up and down before turning back to Zoe. "I scrub up all right for a mom, huh?"

Zoe was about to tell her that she did better than that—and to lead in, she hoped, to broaching the subject of John and that she wanted to linger to talk to him alone once the meal was over—but a pair of chimes rang out in the room, almost at exactly the same time, interrupting them.

Zoe and Shelley exchanged a glance. The sound had come from both of their purses—Zoe's borrowed from Dr. Applewhite to match her dress—their cell phones. There were only two explanations for them both getting a message at the same time. The first was that there was some kind of state – or nationwide emergency and they were being notified by the president.

The second was that they were being called in to work a case.

Zoe prayed briefly for it to be an emergency that wouldn't interrupt their meal, but of course, she didn't believe in God, and any god who heard a prayer from a non-believer would likely go the other way in spite. They fished out their devices, both of them reading the same message: *Call SAIC Maitland ASAP for briefing.*

Shelley sighed. "I guess this night was going just a little too perfectly to be true."

Zoe bit her lip, thinking of John sitting out there waiting for her, and wondering just how many more days it would be now before she got the chance to see him again.

CHAPTER FOUR

Zoe hesitated just outside the squat, square concrete monolith that was the J. Edgar Hoover building. To others, it was ugly, a piece of architecture more reminiscent of Cold War Russia than American greatness. Zoe appreciated its lines and the uniformity of both the interior and the exterior, but she also, at that moment, wished she could be just about anywhere else.

"This is going to be a fun one," Shelley muttered, drawing her light jacket closed a little tighter over her dress.

Zoe, who had not even brought a jacket, was inclined to agree. She was supposed to be talking with John right about now, discussing the future of their relationship and perhaps making decisions that would have given her enough happiness to last a long while. Instead, she and Shelley were about to walk through a whole building full of their colleagues in evening wear and makeup, which sounded just a tiny bit like Zoe's idea of hell.

They were only just in through the doors, waiting for the lift to come, when the first comment was made. Johnson, an agent with a smart mouth on him at the best of times, was swaggering down the corridor toward them. "Hot date, ladies?" he asked, pointing a gun-finger at them. "Good to see you two finally admitting your urges."

Shelley rolled her eyes. "I'm happily married, Johnson. To a man."

"Oh," Johnson said, feigning shock. "I wasn't expecting such homophobia from the Bureau's crack female duo."

"I'm not homophobic, I'm just—" Shelley sighed, closing her eyes for a moment before continuing in a calmer tone. "Not a lesbian. And Johnson? Do me a favor and bite me."

Zoe half-smiled. While it wasn't fun to be ribbed by their colleagues, especially when she didn't understand the references and undertones half of the time, it was kind of fun to see Shelley get flustered by something. It made a change, and while Zoe didn't exactly want Shelley to feel bad, it was a nice reminder that they were both human.

With catcalls and comments about everything from their shoes to their hair trailing them like the contrail behind a pair of jets, they finally made it to the door of SAIC Maitland's office. Shelley took a moment, straightening her shoulders and pushing a loose strand of hair over her shoulder, before knocking.

"Enter."

The man's booming voice was as much a factor in his intimidating presence as his size. At six foot three, Leo Maitland was more than just tall—he was also wide, with fifteen-inch biceps that belied his age. The graying hair at his temples was the only thing pointing to the fact that he was in his mid-forties, with his straight military posture as intact as it had been when he first came out of the army.

"Sir," Zoe and Shelley said, almost in unison. He was the one who had called them there. They knew better than to start in on unnecessary small talk. The Special Agent in Charge of the Washington, D.C. branch was a busy man, and his time was precious.

SAIC Maitland continued looking over a piece of paperwork for a few moments, frowning as he concentrated, before signing it with a flourish and putting it to one side. "Agents Prime and Rose," he said, sifting through an overflowing tray on his desk to pull out a file. "I have a feeling you're going to like this one."

Zoe frowned. Like a murder case? That seemed unlikely, unless the killer was suffocating his victims in cotton candy, and all the clues required vigorous taste-testing. "Sir?" she asked, dubiously.

"That was sarcasm, Agent Prime," he said, his face not cracking a smile. He was holding the file out in one outstretched arm. "Is one of you going to take this, or have you both developed paralysis?"

Shelley sprang forward, taking the case from his hand. "Sorry, sir."

"About this case. Your plane is scheduled for four hours from now," he said, pressing on as if nothing had happened. "Your tickets are inside the file. It was the soonest we could get you booked out to Nebraska."

The word ran through Zoe's spine like a bolt of lightning. Nebraska. Her state of birth. Not that it meant anything—it was a big place. They weren't likely to be anywhere close to where she grew up.

"Two women within the last two days found beheaded. Sounds like it's shaping up to be a serial case, so we need you on the ground as soon as possible. Sorry for the red-eye, but you'll hit town in the early morning and be able to liaise with the local PD as soon as you arrive," Maitland continued. "We have two different kill sites in two different towns, so it's possible the perpetrator may be traveling. You need to get this shut down as quickly as possible. We don't want him traveling out of state and vanishing."

Shelley was leafing through the file, and she winced at some photographs. Zoe, leaning over her shoulder, caught sight of a considerable blood spray before Shelley turned the page.

"We'll try our best, sir," Shelley said, her voice slightly distant, her mind already focused on the file.

"Don't try your best," Maitland said darkly. "There's going to be a lot of press attention on this. Get it solved. Before the whole thing turns into a circus, and I have to explain to our boss why we have a spiraling body count in front of the world's cameras."

❧ ❧ ❧

Zoe held the phone in one hand, trying to balance it against her neck so that she could fold clothes as she spoke. "I really am sorry," she said. "It looks like we may be away a few days at least."

"I knew what I was getting into when we went on our first date," John's voice came from the receiver, his tone light and amused. "It's fine. Save the world. I'll be here when you get back."

Zoe chewed on her lip absently, finishing the last of her clothes and walking quickly to the bathroom to grab her traveling toiletries kit. Her voice echoed off the tile when she spoke. "I hate that I keep having to cut our dates short," she said. "Tonight was fun."

"It was," John said, just before his voice slipped into something a little silkier. "I was looking forward to driving you home. That dress of yours—I appreciated it very much."

Zoe glanced at the red fabric now discarded on top of her bed, and a little thrill pooled in the bottom of her stomach at his words. She tossed the toiletries into her suitcase, casting around for what else need to go in. "Maybe I'll wear it again for you when I get back." Shoes—she threw open the door of her closet and pulled out a spare pair of shoes, just in case the ones she was wearing became uncomfortable.

"I'd like that." John's voice shifted again, this time toward a more serious tone. "Actually, I'd like it if we could have a talk when you're home again."

Zoe hesitated. Talk. What did that mean? Weren't they talking now?

Was this the thing she'd always heard about in movies—the dreaded talk— the moment of the break-up?

No—surely she was only being paranoid. John was an adult. He wasn't afraid to say how he felt, and he hadn't expressed any dissatisfaction so far.

Of course, he couldn't have been happy that she was running off somewhere again right as they seemed to be getting to the good bit.

"Right," Zoe forced herself to say, not wanting the silence to drag on any longer. "Of course. We should do that."

"Call me when you're back, then," John said. He paused, too. "Zoe?"

"Yes?"

There was another pause, as if he was weighing his words. "Have a safe flight."

Zoe stared down at the phone in her hand, the screen now dark, the call ended. For a brief moment she thought that it was absurd—that she wouldn't call him when she got back, wouldn't even think of it. Why would she put herself into a horrible situation on purpose?

But, she reminded herself, she had no idea what he wanted to say. Just because she had come to expect rejection, thanks to her abilities and the way they made her seem different and strange to everyone else, didn't mean he was lining up to give her the same. She thought of Dr. Monk and what she would say—probably something to the effect of not assuming for other people—and tried to clear her head.

A tinkling sound caught her attention as she pulled out a laundry bag to pack inside the suitcase for her dirty clothes. Zoe's hands flew to her ears, and she realized that in all the rush and confusion of getting ready, she hadn't yet taken out her earrings.

She approached the bathroom mirror slowly, the first time she had taken a moment's pause since leaving SAIC Maitland's office. The eyeliner was still flashing over each of her eyes, a reminder of what the night should have been.

With regret, Zoe reached for her facewash and a cloth. The night was over, and there was no point trying to cling to it with a relic that would only smudge across her face when on the plane.

Zoe rubbed her eyes and yawned. It was just around dawn, not that either of them could tell it. They'd left the blind down on their window, leaving the world beyond the plane to the imagination in order to block out the light while they stole a few hours of sleep.

After the mad rush to get changed and into clothing more suitable for travel, to grab her overnight bag, to set up the delayed-release cat feeder and rearrange some appointments, four hours had turned out to be only just enough time for Zoe to meet Shelley back at HQ to go to the airport. Once on the plane they had agreed for the need to get some rest, so that they were actually able to make some kind of sense when they landed.

"All right," she said. "So, after we land, there's a rental car already paid for?"

"Yeah," Shelley confirmed, flipping through the documentation they had been provided. "The Bureau actually sprang for priority collection, so it shouldn't take us long to get on the road."

"And then where to?"

"Says here Broken Ridge," Shelley said, already moving on to the next page.

Zoe's heart thudded in her chest. "Broken Ridge?" she replied, hoping against hope that she had heard incorrectly.

"Yeah, about an hour's drive from the airport," Shelley said, studying the map quickly. "Why?"

Zoe swallowed. "Just checking," she said.

That wasn't the truth. The truth was something that she didn't want to admit: that the town of Broken Ridge was close, uncomfortably close, to where Zoe had grown up. So close that she could picture the place in her head. She knew there was a wind farm not far from the town, a development that had gone up in her youth.

Thoughts and memories of Broken Ridge led, inevitably, to thoughts and memories of home. Not that the place where she grew up had ever been kind enough to her to be called home. *Devil child*, her mother's voice rang in her ears, as clear now as it had been when she was eight years old and cowering next to her bed with her hands clasped together in faux prayer.

Zoe took a breath, counting it out. Three seconds inhale, four seconds exhale. For a moment she almost felt she could feel the warmth of a tropical sun on her face, with her eyes closed, shutting out both the close environs of the plane and the memories crowding in on her.

She opened her eyes, focused and calm again. "What do we have on the victims?" she asked.

"Here," Shelley said, handing her a single sheet of paper. She kept another for herself, and started to read aloud from it. "The first was identified as one Michelle Young, from identification she carried in her pocket. They weren't able to identify her from her face, because her head was missing."

Zoe swore under her breath. "They still do not have it?"

Shelley shook her head no. "There's a recent picture, though. Here." She held up an image of a smiling blonde, looking directly into the camera. There was an arm around her shoulders, though the owner was cropped out. "Looks like it was cut off with something sharp, possibly some kind of sword. Hack marks—the initial assessment is a long blade, possibly a machete. She was in her early thirties. Five nine, one hundred and sixty pounds. No tattoos. She worked as a bank teller. She was the one in the other town—Easterville."

Zoe took her cue when Shelley looked up, done with the details on her report. "I have Lorna Troye," she read. "Her head was missing, too. Thirty-two years old, five seven, one hundred and thirty pounds. Apparently, she was a freelance illustrator. There's a photograph."

The two of them regarded the image of Lorna, taken for the profile page on her own website. She was smiling gently at the camera, though she held a stiff and professional pose. She was holding a pencil in her hand hovering over a sketchpad, as if ready to begin work.

There was a moment of silence between them as they both regarded the dead women. One blonde and one brunette, just like Shelley and Zoe themselves. Zoe was around the right age, too, Shelley a few years younger.

There but for the grace of God, the saying went. But since Zoe had ceased believing in God after she had ceased believing what her mother told her—that she had the devil's blood in her veins to make her see the numbers—she had no idea what it was that made her the lucky one.

"We'll be descending soon," Shelley said, stifling a yawn. "We should get ready."

Get ready, Zoe thought. And how exactly were you supposed to get ready to descend into the one place you had spent your entire adult life trying to escape?

She fastened her seatbelt, knowing that she had little choice.

CHAPTER FIVE

The early morning sun coated everything in a glittering light as Zoe followed Shelley across the parking lot, hanging back with reluctance. She had the itching feeling of being somewhere that was semi-familiar, but that she did not remember well enough to explore with confidence.

Then there was the other feeling at the back of her neck, the one that whispered that she might even end up seeing someone she used to know, this close to home. The parking lot was full of state vehicles—a coroner's van, local sheriff department cars, and the various other officials who would no doubt have flocked with eagerness to a crime of this magnitude in a town so small. It was not the normal order of business for them—which was why it was so important for them to have the assistance of the FBI.

"Sheriff Hawthorne?" Shelley called out, shading her hand with an eye and waving across a line of official warning tape toward a man in shades of brown and beige. He waved in response and began to trudge over, his white hair catching the sun like a halo at the top of his six-foot height.

"You must be the FBI gals," he said, glancing over their regulation FBI-branded windbreakers and black suits. "Body's gone. Had to get it away out of the elements last night. But we've got the crime scene, preserved and ready for you to see."

"I'm Agent Shelley Rose," Shelley said, briefly flashing her badge at him as procedure demanded. "Please, lead the way."

"Agent Zoe Prime," Zoe added, aping Shelley's movements and then turning to follow them both. At least she had never run into this sheriff before. Maybe that boded well for the rest of their visit.

The green grass on either side of the trail fairly sparkled in the morning light, so fresh and scattered with the lightest dew. It was like being inside a postcard, Zoe thought as they stepped along the well-worn path. It was clearly heavily frequented. Zoe noted the growth patterns of the grass around it, where and when it thinned out, how the wide entrance to the parking lot thinned out to a one-person trail, like a tributary moving away from the ocean.

"It was last night she was found?" Shelley was asking, more for confirmation than anything else.

"Late in the afternoon," the sheriff confirmed. "We were alerted by a hiker enjoying the last of the nice weather. They wanted to get up to one of the higher ridges and look back over the town at sunset. Unfortunately, they didn't get very far before they stumbled on Miss Troye's body. She was right on the trail—well, you'll see."

His words were ominous enough, a stark contrast to the idyllic nature of the park and its trails. Zoe cast her eyes from side to side as they walked; up ahead, three men in the same beige and brown uniforms were milling around in a group, no doubt guarding their destination. But around them, to left and right, there was not much to remark upon except for the rolling hills and ridges, shrubbery, and a little further away, the soaring white facades of the wind turbines. Forty-two, she counted at a glance, though there may have been more of them out in the distance where the bright sky would fade them to invisible.

It was the openness that struck her the most. There were no mountains here providing cover, no heavily wooded glades that someone could hide in. There were only the ridges, and the low bushes that clung to them here and there. It wasn't the kind of place that she would choose, if she was going to commit a murder in broad daylight.

"The killer is bold," she said, for Shelley's benefit. "No cover."

Shelley nodded, dropping a step behind the sheriff so that they could talk. "The victim was alone, but not completely isolated. Someone at the parking lot would have been able to see. Maybe not all of the details, but probably enough to know something was going on."

"If the victim screamed, she would have been heard," Zoe added, looking back at the cars now that they were closer to the scene. "Or if she had been able to get away and run, she might have actually escaped. Been able to raise the alarm. This was a big risk."

They approached the sheriff's men, standing in a vague semicircle around an area that they fastidiously avoided. Now that they were close enough to look down on it, Zoe could see why: the ground was saturated with blood. It had soaked into the soil and dyed it red, and the blades of grass still bore individual drops splattered away from the body at the time of the attack.

She dropped into a crouch at the very perimeter of the area that was roped off with more tape, getting her eyes closer to the scene for analysis. Calmly, like opening a gate, she allowed the numbers to come flooding back to her.

The victim, Lorna Troye, had shed her life's blood here. So many pints of it splashed around, and allowing for the soak into the chalky soil, far too much for a person to survive even if her head had not been removed from her neck. It gushed out around one central point, just off to the side of the trail, but the blood also splattered on both sides of the worn path and onto the smooth stones that pebbled it. That told of hacking cuts, enough force to spray those droplets out to either side. Enough to coat shoes and trousers, perhaps even to spray up the front of a shirt.

Zoe circled slowly, still on the outside, not wanting to disturb the evidence any further than it already had been. The path, where it had been worn down, was flat and hard; no footprints were recorded on it, no sign of a struggle. There was a harsh gouge in the earth where the majority of the blood fell, the blade of the murder weapon driving down into the softer soil after the head was severed. The blow had been a strong one.

Did that indicate their killer's superior strength? Maybe. But it was also possible that the attack took several blows. The ME report for the previous victim hinted at a chopping action—the sword coming down again and again until the job was done. Zoe searched closer, using her gloved hands to carefully lean forward and push a few strands of grass here or there.

There—another line, just close to the first, off at a fifteen-degree angle and with a shallower impact by two inches. He had hacked at her neck until it was severed. So, perhaps not freakishly strong, though it still took some good arm power to force the blade through bone and muscle.

"They don't have much," Shelley muttered, rejoining her partner at the side of the tape. "You see anything?"

Zoe stood, feeling the protest in her hamstring muscles as she forced them to move. The numbers were failing her today, with barely any physical evidence to go on. She could estimate the victim's height from the depressions in the grass, but what help was that? They already had her on a slab. "Not much.

Inconclusive on the killer's height, weight, and upper body strength, although I think we can safely say we are not looking for a weakling. Likely a male, to be able to cut off the head. I cannot estimate his physical attributes because he did the decapitation when she was already on the ground."

"They conducted a wider search of the area by grid last night and found nothing of consequence," Shelley said, shading her eyes as she looked over at the rest of the wind farm, stretching out in front of them. "What are you thinking about the location? It's too random a place to just lie in wait for someone to walk by, surely?"

"And the lack of cover," Zoe grunted in agreement. "This doesn't fit into the typical crime of opportunity blueprint. This was something else."

Shelley was biting her lip, looking around. A light breeze stirred the short hairs at her temple, making them stand up. "Why not lie in wait somewhere with more cover, or further into the park?" she said. She sounded like she was thinking aloud, rather than seriously asking the question. "Right here, so close to the parking lot—there has to be a reason why he took the risk."

Zoe looked down at the bloodstains on the floor again. "The body was lying in this direction," she said, pointing with her arms. Feet toward the rest of the park, head toward the parking lot. "Normally when someone is attacked by a concealed predator, it is done from behind, causing the victim to fall forward."

"You're saying that it's likely she was walking back toward the parking lot when it happened."

"Maybe she was leaving. He had to do it now, before the opportunity was gone." Zoe gazed at the nearby cluster of bushes, their leaves speckled with red drops like macabre berries. "Perhaps she did see him, and was running away. But I don't see signs of running—no churned-up ground. She was off to the side, too, away from the harder path. There would be marks on the turf."

Shelley closed her eyes, as if she were visualizing the scene. "So, we have Lorna walking away, back to the parking lot. He looks ahead and knows he only has a short timeframe before she's back to safety and he can't attack. He chooses this moment. Maybe he concealed himself to the side, in those bushes."

Zoe shook her head, measuring the size of the bushes. Not enough coverage. "I do not think so," she said, but there was an easy enough way to prove it. "Deputy?"

One of the young men who had been guarding the site looked up at her call. "Yes, ma'am?"

"Do us a favor. Please go and stand in those bushes just there. Crouch or lie down as if you're trying to hide from view."

The deputy blinked, then looked to his sheriff, who waved a hand of approval. He did as he was told, moving to conceal himself in the bushes. Even though he wore natural colors, it was easy to spot him amongst the vibrant greens. The bushes were low, and the gaps between their forms left little shelter.

Shelley moved around the cordon to the other side of the trail, looking back toward him. "I can see him from here," she confirmed.

"Crouch a little," Zoe called to her. "You are an inch too tall."

Shelley bent her knees temporarily, ducking down well over two inches. "It makes no difference," she said. "I can see his feet and his shoulders."

"Thank you, Deputy. You can get up," Zoe said, much to the relief of the young man, who leapt up and instantly began brushing away leafy debris from his clothing.

"He was walking, then," Shelley said, coming closer to her. "She didn't run, so she probably saw him and didn't think he was a threat."

"Then he can't have been carrying a machete," Zoe pointed out. "Not openly, at least."

"What if he knew the victims?" Shelley asked. Her eyes were back on the town in the near distance. "They're in close proximity. Someone could easily work in one town and live in the other, for example. It would be very plausible for these both to be personal connections."

"Most personal murders are crimes of passion," Zoe said, citing by rote the statistics from the textbooks. Even if she knew that off by heart, there was something the textbooks had never been able to tell her: the atmosphere of a crime scene. Here, maybe, she was finally starting to get it. There was planning here somehow, and only enough cuts to chop off the head—no overkill, no frenzy. Calmness. "This is cold and calculated."

"It could still be personal. Maybe this has been a long and slow mental snap. Maybe he's a psychopath."

Zoe still wanted to flinch whenever she heard that word. It had been flung at her enough times. By her mother, by her peers at school, by anyone who thought she didn't react to social situations with the correct level of emotional response. She had always known she was different. It had taken her a long time to learn that she wasn't evil because of it.

"I see two options," she summarized, pushing the feeling away. "Either he walked past her innocently, then turned and attacked with a concealed blade—or he gained her trust first. That may well have been through a preexisting personal connection, or some other method."

"Then we first have to figure out if Lorna Troye and Michelle Young knew any of the same people," Shelley said. Despite the dark rings around her eyes from the overnight flight, she was beginning to look brighter and more alert. Almost excited at the prospect of a new lead. "Would you like to go see a body?"

Zoe put on a wry smile for her benefit. "I thought you'd never ask."

CHAPTER SIX

The coroner's office could have been any small-town coroner's office in the US, Zoe thought. A cold room with steel tray-beds, just two of them because this place was never particularly busy. One wall lined with nine innocuous drawer handles that nonetheless held unspeakable horrors—at least, to most people. To Zoe and Shelley, it was a Sunday like any other day of the week.

"This is her." The coroner, a paunchy man with near-sighted glasses that turned his face into an owl's, pulled out one of the trays with what seemed like unnecessary force. Zoe felt her muscles tense in anticipation of catching a flying body, but it only rocked slightly on the tray.

The body was covered with a modest white sheet, which ended in a sickeningly empty depression where the head should have been. Zoe reached out and pulled it back, knowing that Shelley was already starting to look a little green.

The sight was arresting. The naked body bore no marks or signs of struggle that she could see in any degree, except for the fact that what had once been the neck was now a stump of messy, hacked-off flesh and fiber. The white bone of the spine was just visible under raw, red meat, cut smoothly and yet with a series of conflicting angles. Each one must have been a separate cut.

"What do you make of it?" Shelley asked softly, her voice low out of respect for a body that could not have heard her even if it was still alive, without the ears to do it with.

"Several strikes across the neck," the coroner said matter-of-factly, pushing his glasses up his nose with one thick finger while the other traced slashes in the air. "Probably a lightweight blade. I'm not able to say with complete certainty, but I would guess a machete. That's what you would normally expect to see."

"Normally?" Zoe asked.

The coroner rolled his shoulders uncomfortably. "Well, I haven't seen anything exactly like this myself," he said. "But I read the statistics. It's more likely a machete than, say, a samurai sword. Though those are probably in second place. People collect them from Japan or get them on the internet."

Zoe resisted the urge to tell him they were called katanas, instead returning to the body. She counted the angles on the neck. Two more than she had seen evidence of at the crime scene, the first two being shallow enough not to have hit the ground. "Can you say how much force was put into the four strikes?"

"Not enough to sever the head in one blow, that's for certain," the coroner said. "You can see the conflicting planes here and here: each time he struck, it was at a slightly different angle, thus causing the rough edge and uneven surface that you see ... four times, yes, as you say."

"Do you think this was someone without natural strength?" Shelley asked, finally recovering enough from the sight to ask a question.

The coroner shrugged. "Without getting into a time machine, it's difficult to say. All I know is the level of force. This could have been an elderly woman hacking with every single shred of her strength running on adrenaline, or it could have been Arnold Schwarzenegger having a lazy day of it. I can't say."

"Not even enough to suggest whether we are looking for a male or a female?"

"Your guess is as good as mine at this stage," the coroner replied. "Your people would be more qualified to answer that question, on the other side of the investigation. Motive, opportunity, et cetera."

It didn't help them much, but it was fair. "We've seen all that we need to," Zoe said, stepping away to allow the man to slide the drawer closed.

"Thank you," Shelley told the man, before following Zoe as she left the room.

Outside, the sun was fully up at last, a brightness that made Zoe dig her sunglasses out of her pocket. The heat was strong, too, bearing down on them like a physical weight. Zoe lingered in the shade cast by the coroner's office, squinting toward their car in the parking lot and calculating exactly how hot it would be inside. The knowledge did not bring any comfort.

"Where to now?" Shelley asked.

"Lorna Troye's family," Zoe said. "See if they can point us in the right direction. Maybe they know something that connects her to Michelle Young."

"According to the file, she doesn't have a lot of family left," Shelley said. It was from memory. She must have read that section already. Zoe felt a guilt low in the pit of her stomach that she hadn't. "Parents were killed in a car accident about ten years ago. She just has one sister left."

Zoe nodded. "All right, then." She thought about it for a moment. Neither of them moved; Shelley was either looking forward to the hot car just as little as Zoe was, or she was giving her space. "We don't really know what we're looking for yet."

"Male or female, strong or not, no idea of physical attributes." Shelley sighed. "It would be great to have a witness pop up sometime soon. What do you think? Any ideas of where to start our profile?"

Zoe shook her head slightly. "Could go either way. The ferocity of the attack would be associated with masculinity in most circumstances. Women, as we know, tend to go for less physical methods of attack. But then again, Lorna Troye clearly wasn't uneasy when she was attacked. She may even have trusted the attacker or felt safe around them. That would potentially suggest a female assailant."

"The thing that strikes me most about the whole thing is the idea of doing it out in the open."

"It smacks of confidence," Zoe said. "That or madness. Some kind of feeling that they weren't going to get caught. Perhaps the cuts lacked power because they weren't in a rush. They felt invincible in that moment. Like the world was pausing to allow them to strike."

"Mm," Shelley agreed, leaning back against the cool stone of the building. "We need to figure out a way to narrow it down some more. Get an idea of what's going on here."

"Then let's hope that Lorna Troye's sister can help us with that," Zoe said, reluctantly stepping out into the full heat of the sun and making for the car.

Lorna Troye's sister lived in a small apartment close to the center of town, above a hardware store. Improbably, the apartment's entrance—which gave a nice view of a stand of hammers—admitted them to a corridor painted in cool yellow, and then a living room which was various shades of pink and mostly velvet.

"Are you sure I can't get you anything?" Daphne Troye, Lorna's older sister, asked for at least the sixth time.

"Really, Ms. Troye, we're fine," Shelley assured her, giving her a bright smile.

"Oh, it's Mrs. Troye." Daphne smiled back, twisting her hand to show them a dully glinting gold band. "My wife took my name when we married."

"Mrs. Troye," Shelley corrected herself. "I know this must be a stressful time for you. We just want to check in with you about a few things to see if we can catch whoever did this to your sister."

The smile on Daphne's lips, already fragile, shattered into small pieces. "Yes," she said, resting fully back in her chair, seemingly accepting that she wasn't going to be getting up to fetch anything. "Of course. Please, ask away."

"What can you tell us about yesterday?" Shelley asked. "Were you in contact with Lorna?"

"A little." Daphne's eyes flitted briefly to a closed room on the other side of the hall from the open door, and then back. "Lorna and Rhona—my wife—don't really get along. We've not been speaking as much, lately. At least, not in person. But I sent her a text in the morning."

"Did you know that she was planning to go out on a hike?"

"Yes." Daphne picked up her own cup, filled with a milky substance that could have been either tea or coffee judging by how diluted it was, and took a tiny sip. "She did tell me. She was supposed to go out with a friend, but they cancelled at the last minute."

"Do you have the name of that friend?" Zoe asked, flipping open her notebook.

"Uh," Daphne paused, pinching the bridge of her nose and screwing her eyes closed as she thought. "Let me just...Cora! Her name was Cora."

"Surname?"

Daphne shook her head. "No, sorry."

"That's all right," Shelley said. "Cora isn't a common name. I'm sure we'll be able to find her from that."

"I would like to show you a photograph, if I may," Zoe said. Seeing Daphne's eyes widen and her hand begin to shake, she quickly added: "Not of the crime scene. Don't worry. This is a photograph of a woman. We just want to ask if you recognize her—particularly, if you have ever seen Lorna with her."

She took the printed photograph of Michelle Young out of the back of her notebook and slid it across the table, letting Daphne get a good look at it.

"I...I don't think so," Daphne said, after a long moment, looking up. "Who is it?"

"Her name is Michelle Young," Zoe said. "Do you recognize that name?"

Daphne shook her head. "Is this...the person that you think did it?"

There was a note of fear in her voice, but also hope. Knowing the perpetrator would be a relief, no doubt. One step closer on the road to understanding why her sister had been taken away. Zoe was sorry that she could not give that to her.

"No, Mrs. Troye," Zoe said, taking the picture back. "We have reason to believe that this woman may be another victim of the same killer."

Daphne half-choked on a breath, looking for a moment like she'd been sucker-punched in the stomach. "It wasn't just Lorna?"

"We can't be one hundred percent sure just yet," Shelley said soothingly, a built-in response from her days in training. Never say anything is for certain until the case is wrapped up. "But there are certain similarities in the crime scenes. It's an avenue that we're exploring."

Daphne swallowed hard, her eyes dropping to the cup in front of her. She didn't say another word. She seemed to be having a hard time processing the information.

Zoe exchanged a glance with Shelley. She had a feeling that this ought to be the end of their interview, and when Shelley gave her a slight nod, she knew she was right. "Thank you, Mrs. Troye," she said. "We'll leave you to it, now. If you think of anything else, please do not hesitate to give us a call."

There was no response from the woman sitting in front of them except for the barest of nods, and an almost imperceptible move up and down of her shoulders. Shelley and Zoe got up, both of them hesitant to leave her—but they knew she was not alone. Away in the room with the closed door, giving them privacy, had to be her wife; they would get through it together.

Though they would be likely to get through it sooner, at least in Zoe's experience, if they had concrete information about who had taken their loved one away from them—and the chance to see justice done.

"We'd better get to the sheriff's station and set up an investigation center," Zoe said, pausing just before she got into their rented car. "The sooner we get a lead on this, the better. Looks like we have someone to start with: the friend, Cora."

"Maybe we'll get lucky," Shelley said, with dark humor. "Maybe she's the one who did it."

But as she got behind the driver's seat, Zoe privately thought that there was no chance at all they were that lucky.

CHAPTER SEVEN

"All right," Zoe said, settling down in front of the table they had set up by pushing two desks together. "What do we have so far?"

Shelley glanced over the files they had spread over both sides of the table. One side for Michelle Young, one side for Lorna Troye. "We have two young women, around the same age. Both murdered during the daytime, which shows a certain level of confidence. Both in the same local area, albeit in two different towns, within the same state. One blonde, one brunette. Both alone at the time of death. Neither with any witnesses."

"And we have the murder weapon appearing to be the same one in both cases," Zoe added. "The machete, used to behead the victims and remove the heads to an as yet unknown location."

Similarities and differences. In the early stages of a case involving multiple homicides, that was what you had to look for. What did the victims have in common, that would single them out and make them targets? What was different between them?

Their age and good looks were a good enough starting point as to the targeting. Opportunity might have come into it, and might not, as they had already explored.

But what about the differences?

"The distance between the towns may be significant. A forty-minute driving window."

"Could be he's local," Shelley said. "Or that he's traveling, I suppose?"

Zoe inclined her head. "Statistics suggest that the majority of multiple murderers strike within a radius of their home. Usually not close enough that they do not feel safe. Far enough away to ease suspicion, but still close enough to be able to move easily. A two-hour radius from both towns might be practical in terms of a suspected catchment area."

Shelley glanced over a map. "Too many places in that radius to consider yet," she said. "We'll need to narrow it down more."

What else could they use?

"Lorna was not supposed to be alone when she was killed," Zoe said out loud, thinking it over. "That means that if our killer was lying in wait for her, he would either have known that her plans were cancelled or would have just been waiting for anyone to drop by without knowing exactly who to expect."

Shelley was biting one of her fingernails, worrying at the side of it with her teeth. "The friend that cancelled," she said. "We should be able to track her down. Do we have Lorna's cell phone?"

"Not as yet," Zoe said, checking over an evidence log that the sheriff had provided them with. "It looks like they have someone trying to get into it. It was password-protected. We will probably have to wait on a warrant for the cell company to provide us with access."

"Social media accounts, then," Shelley said decisively, taking out her own cell and starting to tap around on the screen.

"I am not sure that we have her account names just yet," Zoe said, flipping back and forth through the pages of the report about Lorna's belongings.

"We don't need them," Shelley said, smiling. She held up her screen. On it was clearly displayed an image of Lorna, shown on the feed of a Facebook page. "Not many Lorna Troyes in this area to choose from."

Zoe scooted closer, leaning over the table so she could get a better look. "Any recent posts from a Cora?"

Shelley scrolled down the feed a little. "Yes, here, look: she tagged both of them at a restaurant a couple of weeks ago. Cora Day."

"Good work." Zoe nodded. "I don't suppose we are lucky enough that she has Michelle Young also listed as a friend?"

Shelley frowned, spinning the screen back toward herself and quickly swiping down the page, looking through Lorna's friends list. "No, doesn't look like it."

"Maybe we can see if they have any shared interests or friends other than Cora," Zoe suggested. "I will take Michelle, you stay on Lorna. We can call out the friend names in alphabetical order and see if any match up."

Shelley obliged, going back to Lorna's list and dutifully reading out the names on it one by one. Zoe, who had thankfully been able to find Michelle easily enough by checking out her profile image, kept an eye on the alphabetical list of her friends in turn. None of them matched.

Shelley sighed. "That's a dead end, then."

"Maybe not yet," Zoe cautioned. "This is still a small enough area, and it is not like everyone automatically adds each person they meet to their friends list. We should take a look at their posts and check-ins. Maybe they both go to the same location regularly."

Shelley agreed. "I'll start making a list," she said. "Anything from the last few months. We can compare notes."

Zoe set to work checking out Michelle's feed. It was slow work. Michelle seemed to have had a habit of venting every possible thought on her page, often with such vague commentary that it seemed only the person who it was aimed at would be able to truly understand it. There was often a flurry of comments on these vague updates, asking for more details that Michelle never gave.

But, wait: there . . . was that . . . ?

"Cora Day?" Zoe said, out loud. "That was her name?"

"That's right," Shelley said, looking up. "Do you have something?"

"Here," Zoe said, showing her. "Looks like they did know each other after all."

There was a photograph, showing Michelle and a group of other women. Standing off to the left, and smiling, was a woman tagged as Cora Day.

"That's her," Shelley confirmed. "Where was that taken?"

Zoe consulted the tags. "At a nightclub in town. I'll keep looking. There may be more."

There was more, and it didn't take her long to find it. There, just a few posts below, was a comment from Cora—the first she had seen, but in chronological terms, the most recent.

Whatever had been going on between the two of them, it did not seem to have been pleasant.

"Listen to this," Zoe said, reading aloud. "You're so obvious, bitch. Stop posting updates about me. If you want to say something, say it to my face."

"What's that?" Shelley gasped.

"That is a comment from Cora Day on Michelle Young's Facebook wall," Zoe said triumphantly. "It looks like they were friends until this moment.

Michelle tells her to screw herself and then Cora never replies. I imagine that's the point where they blocked one another."

"How long ago was that?" Shelley asked, thoughtfully.

Zoe consulted the timestamp. "Just over a month ago."

"So, to recap," Shelley said, a smile slowly forming on her face, "Cora Day falls out with Michelle Young, and around a month later she ends up dead. Then Cora cancels on meeting up with Lorna Troye for a pre-planned hiking trip, leaving her alone, and Lorna also ends up dead by the same method."

"And the coroner says that it is altogether possible the suspect we are looking for could be a woman, especially given the extra boost of adrenaline that might allow them to strike with more strength than expected."

"Plus the fact that the killer was confident enough to approach both women in daylight when they were alone, without having them running in fear, quite likely because they already knew them."

"Looks like we have a suspect," Zoe said, catching the excitement that Shelley obviously felt. And why not, after all? This could be it—the lead that was going to blow the whole case open.

"I'll talk to the sheriff about a current address for Cora Day," Shelley said, jumping out of her chair and rushing along the corridor with newfound enthusiasm.

CHAPTER EIGHT

Zoe eyed the building from the driver's seat of their rental car, looking up to the third floor and the rooms where Cora Day was registered as living. It wasn't a bad area, and the apartment building was actually an older converted home, split into three floors with each one serving as a self-contained unit.

"So far, so suburbia," Zoe said, glancing up and down the street. There were short manicured patches of lawn here and there, trees growing out of the sidewalk at measured junctures, and even a bona fide white fence across the street. Still, it wasn't as though murders only happened in rough and ready poor communities. They were quite capable of popping up anywhere at any time—if she had learned anything in her years with the FBI, it had to be that.

"Well, appearances can be deceptive," Shelley said, echoing her own thoughts as she got out of the car. "What are we expecting here?"

Zoe shrugged, joining her on the sidewalk and fastening up the button on her suit jacket. "I find it safest not to expect anything. If Cora is a psychotic killer, there is no telling how she might react to our request for a conversation. She may try to run. To lie to us. She may even threaten violence. And on top of that there is still always the possibility that she will go quietly, admit to everything, and allow us to get on a plane home before dinnertime."

"That might be wishful thinking," Shelley said, giving her a lopsided grin.

"It well might," Zoe said, sighing and taking the first step toward the building. It never got easier, the feeling of going in to approach a suspect for the first time. The tension and nerves, the hope that you were right and the case was solved, often coupled with a dismay that someone so normal-seeming could really be a cold-blooded killer. Above all of that was the kind of fear that usually lurked around every case: that any stop you might make along the way could put you into contact with a violent criminal, one who would not think twice about shooting down or bludgeoning an agent of the law.

A fear that, Zoe noticed, had been growing proportionately the closer she got to John and Shelley and the further away she got from the numbers.

On the third floor of the building, against a stairwell that had been awkwardly converted to include lockable front doors for each apartment, Zoe knocked and waited. Her hand strayed to her gun, resting in a holster. Just the touch of the handle was reassurance enough. There was no sense in drawing it when all you intended to do was interview a potential suspect. There was such a thing as inviting conflict, after all.

The door opened onto a sight that Zoe had not expected: a woman, clearly Cora from the photographs yet some tired, faded, pale version of her, wrapped in a large fluffy robe and with red and patchy skin around her nose and cheeks. "Yes?" she asked, her voice nasal and stiff.

"Cora Day?" Zoe asked. Her hand moved, going to the inside pocket where she kept her badge.

"Yes? Who are you?"

Zoe drew out the badge, sensing more than seeing Shelley do the same by her side. "Special Agent Zoe Prime with the FBI. This is my colleague, Special Agent Shelley Rose. We would like to have a word with you, if we may."

"Is this about Michelle?" Cora asked, not sounding surprised at all. She stepped back to allow them inside. "I heard about it from a friend. It's horrible. We were arguing, but I would never have wished for something like this to happen."

"We did hear about the issues between you two," Shelley said, following Zoe and Cora through into a cramped but well-decorated living area. "Could you talk us through what happened?"

"Oh, god, it was so stupid," Cora said, sniffing and settling down into an overstuffed armchair as she indicated for them to take the sofa. "It seems really childish now. It was just about a stupid Facebook game we were playing."

Zoe, settling down onto the comfortable sofa, raised an eyebrow. "A game?"

"Yeah. After she added me it turned out we both play this game, where you run a food stall and sell food to your customers. You can decorate your stall and serve lots of different types of cuisine, and—well, anyway, your friends can send you items if you request them. I had this rare item that Michelle needed in order to complete her event set, which you can only do when the event is on, but I gave it to one of my other friends instead. Then she put up this catty status about playing favorites and I called her on it, and she blocked me. Just like that." Cora shrugged and reached for a tissue from a box in the middle of the table. "Not that it was a huge loss—we barely knew each other. But it was a shock to hear she's dead."

Zoe's ears pricked, catching the words that Cora had used. "You barely knew one another?" she asked.

"We're just friends of friends," Cora said. "I met her once—sorry, excuse me." She broke off to sneeze, catching it in the tissue in her hand and then blinking.

"Are you unwell, Ms. Day?" Shelley asked. It wasn't a difficult assumption to come to: on top of the robe, the red nose, and the sneeze, the coffee table was littered with discarded tissues, and there was a store-brand packet of flu remedy left empty amongst them.

"I've got this blasted cold," she said, breaking off to blow her nose gently. She winced as she did it, the raw, red skin getting another scraping. "It's kept me home all weekend. I was supposed to go out with a friend, and I've just been laying here on the couch."

Zoe and Shelley exchanged a look.

"Yesterday, was it?" Zoe asked.

"Yes. Why?"

"You were supposed to go on a hike with Lorna Troye. Is that not correct?" Zoe said, ignoring the question.

"Yes. I—wait, have you been tracking me or something? I didn't do anything to Michelle, really I didn't—"

"We haven't been tracking you," Shelley cut in. "Cora, we're here because yesterday afternoon, Lorna Troye went out on a hike on her own. Her body was discovered later in the day. I'm afraid that she, too, has been killed."

There was a long pause, and Cora drew in a sharp, gasping breath after it had passed. Zoe realized that she had stopped breathing at the moment the news was delivered. Tears were in her eyes, now, and when she grabbed for a new tissue, it was to dab at them rather than at her nose. "What happened?" she asked, her voice shaky and broken.

"We have reason to believe that she was attacked and killed, just the same as Michelle was," Shelley said. There was a grim set to her tone, and it left no doubt as to what was coming next.

"What...?" Cora asked dimly, looking between the two of them with what seemed to be a growing awareness of the situation. "You can't think that I...?"

"At the present moment, Ms. Day, you are the one thing that links these two women together," Shelley said firmly. "We are going to need you to think very hard, now, and cast your mind back to Friday. We need you to tell us where you were, and who can verify that."

"I was at work," Cora said, her eyes almost popping out of her head. "I was feeling under the weather already, but I thought I'd better go in. Only one day left to the weekend, and all that. So I went in."

"And you were there all day?" Zoe pressed, opening her notebook. "We will need the name and address of your employer, so that we can verify this."

"Yes, I left just after six," Cora said. "I swear, I didn't have anything to do with any of this. I—I didn't even know Michelle, and Lorna was one of my best friends. I would never do anything to hurt..." Cora trailed off, her eyes falling down to her hands as a couple of fat tears rolled down her cheeks unchecked.

"You were saying that you only met Michelle once?" Zoe prompted.

"Yes, that's right. A group of us went out a month ago and Michelle happened to be there. I recognized her from Facebook but we didn't even talk. We just have mutual friends. I think we posed for a few pictures together in a group, but there were others there I didn't know as well. That was after the whole game thing, so I didn't go introduce myself to her. I stayed to one side, did the pictures, carried on talking to my friends."

"And if we speak to the friends you were with that night?" Zoe asked, one eyebrow raised pointedly.

"They'll tell you the same th-thing," Cora said, her breath hitching as she began to sob. "I should have—I should have gone out yesterday with Lorna. Then she'd be fine. Oh, god. Why was I so lazy? She told me fresh air might be good for a cold and I ignored her—I should have gone with her..."

"We don't know that, Ms. Day," Shelley said, gathering herself and standing up. "There's every possibility that, had you been there with her, you might have ended up dead as well. It's not your fault."

"We have everything we need for now," Zoe said, standing up alongside her partner. "But we will leave you this card. If you think of anything that seems suspicious at all—someone new in Lorna's life, any suspicion she might have had of being followed, anything that stands out in any way—please don't hesitate to give us a call."

"I can't think of anything like that," Cora said, sniffling through her tears as she reached out to take the card with a trembling hand. "There was nothing going on. Lorna was just a normal woman. Kind. Talented. Just a good friend."

"Just in case you remember," Zoe said again, then followed Shelley as they let themselves out of the apartment and the building, leaving Cora to succumb to noisy, snotty tears on the sofa.

"That was a dead end," Shelley said, as they paused outside on the street. "No pun intended."

"Mm." Zoe put her sunglasses back on, glancing up and down the street. No inspiration appeared to be forthcoming. "Assuming the alibi checks out, which it probably will, we cannot keep her as a suspect."

"Which leaves us with one big question." Shelley sighed, leaning against the car door and immediately yelping and drawing her hand back from the hot metal.

"Who actually did do it?" Zoe filled in for her, giving her a wry smile as she tentatively went for the door handle herself.

CHAPTER NINE

He glanced at his reflection in a store window as he passed, smoothing down a tiny flyaway piece of hair and checking that everything else was in place. He looked good, which was, of course, by design. You didn't simply get out of bed and roll across town to meet your girlfriend. You made an effort. If you didn't respect yourself enough to make an effort, then why should she?

He resisted the urge to hum a happy tune as he walked down the street, strolling along by familiar sights on his route. He was in a good mood. A very good mood, in fact. That last one had been so good—so sweet. The way she had looked up at him, such fear in her eyes as he swung down the machete...

Ah! It was just like the first time, all over again. He had assumed that this would be much like any other experience—very difficult to recapture that joy and ecstasy and surprise of the first time. Of course, the element of surprise was dying away as rapidly as the women, but the joy—the ecstasy—yes, that had been there. She had been a good choice, that hiker. That blonde hair that pooled around her head as she lay on the ground, silently begging him not to kill her—delicious.

There was a flower store on his route, one that he had passed more than a few times. The air was fresh and the sun was out, and he was feeling good—why not stop in? He pulled off his sunglasses and stepped inside the cool interior, casting a glance over the various bouquets arranged in buckets by color and type.

"Can I help you?" a bored teenage attendant asked him, barely looking up from her phone for long enough to notice him.

He looked up and took her in. "Yes, actually," he said. "I'm just picking out a bouquet. Which one do you suppose is the most romantic?"

48

The teenager flicked her eyes up to his, her expression smoothing out just a little as she looked at him properly for the first time. "Probably roses."

"Roses?" He laughed. "We can do better than that, can't we? Something a bit less obvious?"

She bit her lip momentarily, casting a doubtful eye over the display. "Um. Maybe this one. All the flowers are different shades of pink and red."

He cocked his head, thinking it over. "Yes, that will do nicely," he said. "How much are they?"

"Eight dollars and ninety-seven cents," she said, reading off the label. She was obviously new—not experienced enough to have learned the prices yet.

He held out a crisp ten-dollar bill. "Keep the change," he said, then winked and lowered his voice conspiratorially. "And don't tell your boss."

The teenager flushed slightly, putting his money in the till and drawing out a dollar. She slipped it into her pocket, watching him all the while with a slightly guilty look, but empowered by his permission.

He left the store and carried on down the street, smelling the flowers as he went. They were delightful. Fresh and fragrant, like a spring day on a picnic blanket. The girl had a good eye, even if she didn't know it yet.

There was a spring in his step, a pep and bounce that made him almost want to cartwheel down the street. He smiled and nodded at an older lady walking with a cane, surprising her into returning it. She looked like the kind of woman who had fallen out of the habit of smiling at younger people. A shame. If he'd had the time, he would have stopped and helped her with her shopping, shown her that they weren't all bad.

Still, he couldn't keep her waiting. His lady love. He took another sniff of the blooms, cradling them carefully in his arms to be sure that they wouldn't get crushed. He would do the movie trope gag, he decided—hold them behind his back when she answered the door and then pull them out as a surprise. Until the last minute, she wouldn't know whether he was going to pull out the flowers or a knife. Oh, how they would laugh! He imagined her clutching her cheeks in joy, gabbling on about finding a vase and some water, setting them up in pride of place on the table. Then he'd know he was in her good books, every time he looked over and saw the flowers.

He wondered who would be his next. He was always on the lookout, always eagerly waiting. He was expecting to be able to find out soon—after all, two in a row was a new rush for him, and he didn't want it to end. Perhaps the afternoon was going to bring some new kind of fun. He hoped for it—wished for it. He was still riding this high, and he didn't want it to end.

He daydreamed as he walked, trying to picture another woman who would fall victim to his machete next. Perhaps she would be a blonde again. He did enjoy doing the blondes the most. Some little blonde who would be completely unaware until he was right upon her.

"Afternoon," he called out cheerfully to a man who was just coming out of a nearby door, one of his girlfriend's neighbors. "Nice day, isn't it?"

The man looked around, startled—as everyone always seemed to be—to be addressed by someone in the street. What was the world coming to, that such simple social niceties had been almost utterly discarded. "Lovely day," the man agreed. "You have a good one."

He tipped his hand into the air, acknowledgment and thanks rolled into one, as he arrived at the doorstep. He pressed the buzzer and waited, humming to himself, just remembering at the last minute to stick the flowers behind his back to hide them.

CHAPTER TEN

Zoe swore as they rounded a bend and reached up to adjust the shade across the windshield, swinging it around to cover the driver's side window. The sun was brutal, hot despite the air conditioning turned on full blast inside their rental car, and so bright that she was squinting through her sunglasses.

"I forgot how bad it gets this time of year," she muttered.

"It's not that different from D.C.," Shelley said mildly. "There's a heatwave on across the country right now. I think you have to turn left up ahead."

Zoe knew where she needed to turn, though she held back from saying as much. This place was bringing back too many memories. She'd traveled this road before, remembered the twists and turns the way her mind always grabbed onto patterns and distances. The town of White Arrow was up ahead, less of a destination than Broken Ridge with fewer stores and amenities, but still a thriving settlement in its own right. The population was around 2,500; a smaller number than they were used to dealing with in most cases, but still a sobering reminder that, for now, almost all of that figure added to their potential suspect pool.

Zoe turned left, slowing the pace of their vehicle as they moved away from the highway into the populated center. A few stores lined the road, a school, a library. A parking lot bustling with occupants, a few restaurants. Zoe passed all of it by; they had already arranged to meet Sheriff Hawthorne at the first murder scene, Michelle Young's own home.

"It's busy," Shelley noted. "Busier than I expected."

Zoe glanced down at the GPS, programmed for the exact address they wanted. "It will thin out." She knew this area, knew what it would be like once they'd gotten out past the hub of the town.

Shelley didn't comment on the fact that she was right as they pulled away from the stores and visitors and into a more residential area. Here, there was space between buildings. Yards were wide even when the houses were small. The one thing there always seemed to be an abundance of in Nebraska was space, unless you were a teenage girl cloistered away with your psychotic mother for most of each day, waiting for the moment you could finally make your escape.

Zoe pushed away the dark clouds of her past as she pulled up the car onto the sidewalk outside a neat two-story property with a closely manicured front yard and yellow-painted door. The parking space outside the home was already occupied—first with an unremarkable sedan, and behind it, the sheriff's car. Evidently, he was already waiting for them.

Opening the car door, Zoe stepped out into the full heat of the day. She hated this. Summers always made her think of the worst times of her life: stuck with her mother for long months, without friends to play with, without at least the diversion of school—even if that had never been a place of particular welcome, either. The heat oppressive in their small home, the A/C not always working. Reading textbooks by the light of a candle because her dad had lost his job again and got drunk and walked out, and the cool of the night the only time of welcome relief.

Exactly the kind of memory that would do her no good here, when she needed to focus on the crime scene and learn what she could to stop a killer from striking again.

Shelley joined her on the sidewalk, both of them glancing up and down the neighborhood. There was only an empty space opposite, the houses here built in such a way that no one had to feel particularly close to their neighbors, alternating at spread-out distances. Zoe noted someone watching from the upstairs window of the nearest house on the left side, hanging out on the windowsill to get a breath of air, the light glinting off their spectacles. The distance was far enough that she wasn't tempted to yell to get their attention. That would be why, despite the fact that Michelle Young was murdered in the middle of the day, the sheriff had as yet turned up no witnesses at all.

The front door was propped open by a large white stone, apparently painted that color. Zoe glanced down at the edging of the property and noticed where a line of matching stones ended in an abrupt disturbance of brown earth against the green turf, no doubt pried out by one of the sheriff's men to stop the place from locking.

Without discussing it, Zoe and Shelley walked inside. They needed to examine the property—the whole of it, in case there was further evidence inside. "Sheriff Hawthorne?" Zoe called out, pushing the door aside and stepping into the cooler shade of the hall.

She breathed a sigh of relief momentarily. It was nicer in here. The air was still warm as it lingered near the doorway, but the interior of the house was cool, shades still drawn over most of the windows. It was darker, and her eyes took a moment to fully adjust, but it was not dim enough that she would be tempted to draw open the shades. The sheriff stepped out of the kitchen, his white hair slicked down to his head with sweat when he lifted his hat in greeting.

"Ladies," he said. "Come in. You have anything you want me to guide you towards?"

Zoe shook her head. "We will take a look at everything in turn."

The sheriff shrugged his broad shoulders. "All right. Well, I'll be out in the backyard. We've marked out the scene there for you."

"I'll come with you," Shelley volunteered, stepping forward. "Best that we take a look now so you can get back to your office and some shade. Doesn't do any good to be standing around in this weather."

Zoe hesitated, holding back. The thought of going back out there again so soon made her want to scream. The heat felt like it was pushing her skull tighter together, crushing all the brain cells inside it. "Maybe we should wait," she suggested, knowing even as she did that she had no logical excuse to follow it up with.

Shelley turned, giving her a quick smile. "Don't worry. You stay inside and take a look around. I know you're uncomfortable out there. We can swap later when you've cooled down a bit. For now, you try and think like me and I'll try and think like you. Might be fun."

"You don't mind the heat yourself?" the sheriff asked conversationally, leading Shelley back out toward an open kitchen area flooded with light from the windows facing the backyard.

"Not at all. I'm an Arizona gal," Shelley replied. After that, the door closed behind them, and Zoe was left alone in the cool and the quiet.

She waited a moment, holding her hands against her temples, pushing the heels of her palms down. She needed to get a grip. She took a few brief moments just to breathe, counting her exhales, taking herself away to the paradise island that Dr. Monk had helped her to build as a mental refuge. It was warm there, not oppressively hot. When she opened her eyes again, she felt clearer, more ready to think.

The house was neatly kept. Zoe looked around and saw nothing out of place: no dirty dishes in the sink, no clothes waiting to go into the laundry. The magazines on the coffee table were arranged by size and aligned precisely at their bottom right corners in an orderly pile. *Think like Shelley*, she told herself: the owner of the home was fastidious, house-proud, liked things to be clean and tidy.

More than that: nothing was out of place, which meant there was no struggle here. Nothing knocked aside by accident.

She might have considered the possibility that it was the killer who had tidied up to remove evidence, but the whole home was the same on both floors. There was one place in the bathroom where something looked newly removed: a faint patch of discoloration on a shelf, the white-painted wood slightly more yellow in one spot, perhaps where something had stood for a long time until recently. There was no sign of struggle there, though, and no sign of other disturbance. With the other valuables in the house still on proud display, Zoe couldn't imagine it had been stolen. More likely, the victim had thrown away or moved a knickknack a short while before her death.

In the victim's bedroom, Zoe found her pajamas folded into a neat square on the covers. She let her hand stray out and touch the soft cotton for a moment, well-washed to the point of comfort. Michelle Young, whoever she was, liked things to always be in their right places.

She had chosen her décor and furniture with the same approach. Absolutely everything that could be oak was oak, with the same tone in the wood, the same treatment. Each room had its own color scheme: pale pink in the bedroom, pale blue in the bathroom, sunny yellow through the hallways to match the front door, green in the living room. The kitchen was silver, from the tiles on the floor that had a pale, creamy quality to the stainless steel appliances and the handles of knives and pans hung from hooks on the wall.

Zoe examined the hooks closely, looking for a telltale sign that something was missing. All of the spaces appeared to be filled. It would have been too convenient, she thought, if the killer had taken Michelle Young's butcher knife and cut off her head with it.

She glanced out the window, to where Shelley and the sheriff were standing around a rectangle of yellow hazard tape pegged out with metal stakes. They were both shaking their heads, looking down at the ground. Zoe could make out a faint red marking and nothing more. Most likely, she thought, exactly the same as they had found at the scene of Lorna Troye's death. She had already seen the crime scene photos, which were taken when Michelle was still on the ground. Or, what was left of her. The head, of course, still had not turned up.

Zoe scanned the kitchen again. The cupboards and the hooks on the wall were arranged perfectly for someone who was five nine, which, of course, Michelle had been. At her vantage point of one inch taller, Zoe was able to see things from a little higher than the owner—

No, she told herself. Stop thinking of numbers. Think like Shelley. What would Shelley see here? She would be looking for clues about the person who lived here—about how they had lived, how they might have been surprised, why they were chosen as a target. Not their physical attributes.

Zoe paused beside the refrigerator. Though every effort had been taken, the shining steel surfaces took on marks and smudges more easily than the oak wood, especially after having been polished. The handles of each door held a few such marks, as did the broad surface next to them, where five tips of five fingers had pushed them closed. Zoe squinted closer, and saw the signature trace of a few remnants of white powder. Good: the local forensics team had spotted and dusted the prints already.

She moved across to the stove, made of the same material and polished until it shone in the same way. Here, too, were signs of use. A hand smudge on the handle, a circular mark around one of the knobs on the stove where it had been turned on and then off with a trailing thumb. Zoe leaned down to breathe across the surface, watching her breath turn into a cloud of mist across the surface that quickly dissipated. Like that she could not only make out the fingerprints more clearly, but even the lines left by a sponge or cloth the last time it was cleaned.

The dishwasher, too, was the same steel, even from the same manufacturer. But—Zoe leaned closer, until her eyes were only centimeters from the handle of the machine. There wasn't a mark on it. Perhaps it had not been used since the last cleaning session.

On a whim, Zoe slipped on a pair of evidence gloves and opened the dishwasher, pulling the door away and down. Inside, the machine was bone dry, all of the racks empty. She took a deep sniff of the air inside and smelled nothing. No dishwasher tablets, no cleaning fluid, no old food swept off the plates and gathered inside the filter to slowly rot.

Even for a woman who kept her house clean, that was a little too much.

Shelley and Sheriff Hawthorne were making their way inside as Zoe stood, closing the dishwasher back up. "Is this new?" she asked, directing her question toward the older man.

He screwed up his face for a moment. "Possibly so. I've got a deputy back at the station right now combing through her bank records. If it was a new purchase, he'll flag it up in the report."

"I'll give him a call," Shelley said quickly, pulling out her cell phone. "What's his name?"

Shelley stepped off to the side a moment, making the call. In the meantime, awkward silence lingered between Zoe and the sheriff.

"If it was new, she did not even get the chance to use it," Zoe mused, her eyes going to the knives hanging on the wall. And the point was, they were hanging on the wall—clean. Michelle Young couldn't possibly have had the dishwasher very long if she had no dirty dishes, and yet it hadn't been used.

The sheriff shook his head sympathetically. "What a waste," he said. "Still. Might add a little resale value to the home. Give a little balance to the hit it'll take after having someone die here."

Ghoulishness. Zoe shook her head, mimicking the sheriff, though her sentiment was one of disbelief. People not wanting a house because someone had died there—it was stupid. There was no such thing as ghosts, or psychic energy, or bad luck. She would quite happily have paid market value for this kind of place. Good news for her, anyway, if such a bargain ever did come up at a time when she was looking to buy.

Shelley stepped back toward them, ending the call. "Confirmed. It was ordered and paid for last week. Must have been installed since then."

"A new installation means that a stranger was in the house recently." Zoe noted the obvious, to a nod from the sheriff. It was a potential lead.

"This brand is fairly popular," Shelley said, frowning. Of course—the one area in which Zoe couldn't even fake thinking like Shelley. Knowing the trends and customs that shifted and changed in the cultural conception like so much seaweed in the current. Something Zoe had never been good at keeping up with. If she needed new appliances, she would read up on their statistics and dimensions, not which celebrity endorsed them.

"Is that an issue?" Zoe asked, realizing belatedly that Shelley looked concerned by the fact.

"Well," Shelley said. "A popular brand makes it more likely that others in the area might also have appliances from the same range. I'm just wondering if the next victim recently had an installation of her own. Lorna Troye."

The sheriff took the hint, flipping through the pages of his notebook quickly to check back on what they had found at the other scene. "According to her sister, she just recently got a new dryer. It was a few weeks before the murder, though. We had flagged it up as a possible avenue for investigation after exhausting any other, more likely leads."

"What's the brand?" Shelley asked.

The sheriff looked harassed. "I didn't note it down," he said, dragging his cell phone out of his pocket. He retreated a few steps, putting it to his ear.

"What are we thinking?" Shelley asked. "That he killed Michelle after he'd finished the installation?"

"He would have needed her to sign off on the paperwork. It wouldn't be smart, either. Killing someone at a time when you were registered at their address by your employer. He may have come back later, told her there was something he forgot to fix." Zoe cast her eyes around the kitchen again. "She either went out into the backyard willingly with him, or he surprised her there. Again, with nothing to hide behind. He could not have approached without being seen unless she was utterly distracted."

"Come take a look," Shelley suggested, drawing Zoe out the back door and into the yard.

The fence marking the outlines of the property would have been easy enough to climb over, Zoe thought, but not without noise. The tape-enclosed area was much as she had expected: hard earth, dry from the season, with no marks of footprints or particular scuffing. The blood, soaked into the ground as before, splattered across blades of green grass. The impression in the turf, still faintly visible, of where Michelle Young had lain for long hours before being discovered.

Zoe recalled the case notes. She had been found by a family member who had a key to the property and an arrangement to meet that evening. Were it not for that, she might not have been found for days—even weeks, if her workmates didn't raise the alarm.

There was nothing here. Just two sharp grooves in the earth, one an inch deeper than the other and at a ten-degree angle, a few centimeters apart on one side. Blood had spilled thickly into them, filling them up and staining the ground. Multiple chops with the machete. Boldness. A curious sense of calm despite the bloodshed. All of the signatures of the other scene were here too. There was no doubt that this was the same killer, but what did he want? Why was he choosing these women? What connected them in his mind?

"It was the same manufacturer," the sheriff announced grimly, coming out to stand behind them. Zoe eased to a standing position, feeling the heat already beginning to burn through the suit jacket she wore. "And the same store that sold both devices—it's a national homeware chain, with several stores scattered across the county."

"Give me the branch number," Shelley said immediately, dialing it as the sheriff read it out from an internet search page. They all three waited for the call to connect, Zoe and the sheriff just about holding their breath to try to hear the voice that answered.

"Hello, this is Special Agent Shelley Rose from the FBI," she said rapidly, giving only a brief pause for the employee on the line to take the information in. "We're chasing down information on an ongoing case. I'm wondering if you can help by telling me some details about a couple of recent installations?... Mhmm, that's right. Yes... Fantastic, thank you. Okay, the first one is for a Michelle Young." Shelley rattled off the address and dates for both Michelle and Lorna, nodding and making affirmative noises while she scrabbled in her pocket for her notebook. Zoe, sensing the urgency, dug hers out instead and offered it up.

Shelley stopped abruptly halfway through writing something down, her eyes flicking up to meet Zoe's with a significant look. "You're sure?... Yes. All right, thank you very much. You've been extremely helpful. If you could send a copy of those order details to the sheriff's office, that would be wonderful. Right. Thanks again."

Zoe waited with bated breath as Shelley ended the call, straightening up and looking at them with a grave expression. "They were both dispatched and installed by the same man," she announced.

If Zoe had been a rabbit, her ears would have pricked up and swiveled toward her. "The same man?"

"Bob Taylor." Shelley tapped the page of Zoe's notebook where she had written it down.

The sheriff's mouth was a grim line, held firmly together. "I know Bob. Older guy, been with the company for years. He does a lot of the installations around these parts because he knows how to work with just about every machine on the books. Done a couple of deliveries for me, even."

"Current whereabouts?" Zoe asked, dispatching with any notion or pretense at pleasantries in the face of urgency.

"He's on a job," Shelley said. "It's back in Broken Ridge."

"I'll call my boys and dispatch them to the address. We should move now, if we want to join them," the sheriff said, reaching for the radio on his chest and starting to bark instructions into it.

Without a word, Zoe and Shelley rocketed through the house to their rental car, waiting for the sheriff to pull out first so that they could follow him at high speed behind his siren and lights.

"Hey!" Zoe yelled, only just managing to put the car into park as she leapt out of the driver's seat. "What's going on?"

"Ma'am." It was one of the three men who had been at the Lorna Troye site yesterday—the young one who had lain down behind the bushes when they asked him to. He alone was standing, his hand on the weapon at his hip, watching as two of his colleagues wrestled to keep a cuffed man pinned to the ground. "We had to take action. Suspect was combative and belligerent."

Zoe thought that belligerent was maybe a long word for this group, though she said nothing to the effect. "This is Bob Taylor?" she asked. She had to raise her voice; the man on the ground was swearing and spitting, and the two men holding him down were shouting at him to stay down.

"Yes, ma'am."

"All right, get him up," the sheriff barked. "Enough of this. I want a full report."

The young man stepped forward to help, three of them lifting Bob Taylor bodily from the ground until he could get his feet under him. His face was red and his clothes were dusty from the sidewalk where they had thrown him, a dark blue uniform bearing the name of the store embroidered over a breast pocket. He was fifty-four years old, Zoe estimated, five seven, probably around a hundred and eighty pounds. He was filling out around the middle in his age, his hair cropped close and graying, his face lined from the sun.

All in all, he looked fairly average. He resisted little as the local boys pushed him into the back of a sheriff's department vehicle, one of them sliding in next to him to keep him honest.

"We arrived about five minutes ago," the young deputy was saying, addressing Sheriff Hawthorne. Zoe and Shelley listened in, keeping close. A few yards away, the homeowner was watching from her front doorway, one hand over her mouth. "Knocked on the door and asked Mrs. Goodwell if she had a man on the property conducting an installation. She led us into the kitchen, where we found suspect Bob Taylor working on a washer-dryer. He came out from behind it when we asked for his identity, and having confirmed it, we asked him to come with us to answer some questions."

"How the hell did you get from that to the sidewalk?" Sheriff Hawthorne demanded.

"He became verbally abusive, sir. Started to call us all the curse words under the sun, talking about a job quota and a schedule. I indicated to him that it was better he come with us willingly rather than us having to arrest him. He told us he wasn't going nowhere to no station and tried to push his way out of the room." The deputy cleared his throat briefly. Zoe wondered how much of his side of the story had been embellished. "McWillard tried to stop him by catching hold of his arm, and he became aggressive. We had to drag him out here to stop him from trashing the place up. Then he wouldn't submit to cuffs so we had to take him down."

The sheriff eyed him balefully. He looked as though he believed even less of the story than Zoe did. "Made a scene of it, too. All right. Get him back to the station. We'll follow and put him in for questioning."

"We will take lead on that," Zoe put in quickly. "He will no doubt respond better to someone who hasn't just tackled him to the ground."

The sheriff grunted unhappily, but he didn't disagree. "Fine. Let's just get him back first."

Zoe got one more look at Bob Taylor, sitting in the back of the car, before she and Shelley returned to their own vehicle. He didn't much look like a serial killer—not that there was a particular look they had. Still. He didn't fit the trend. He was far older than most multiple murder suspects, especially where the victims were unconnected to the killer's personal life; someone his age was more likely to kill a wife than a stranger. At the very least, a sex worker. Of course, trends were hardly rules. There were those who broke the curve.

"What are you thinking?" Shelley asked as she strapped in her seatbelt, obviously picking up on Zoe's mood.

"I'm not sure," Zoe admitted, starting the engine. "Just that I don't have a totally good feeling about this."

CHAPTER ELEVEN

Ivy switched off the car engine, heaving a sigh of relief. It was good to be home at last. This heatwave sweeping the country was doing no one any favors, and she prayed it would end—and not just because it was uncomfortable.

Her eyes swept across the fields, the corn stalks tall and almost impenetrable to the eye, a tall mass that started at an unnatural straight line and then dominated her view. The road leading up past them was dusty and dry, and the timbers of the barn in front of her were sun-bleached. The quicker this heat was over the better. The corn would be ready to harvest in a matter of weeks, and Ivy wasn't looking forward to dealing with the farmhands complaining about the sun and slacking off work.

She flipped open the mirror in her sunshield and examined her face quickly, checking her skin. She was showing freckles that came out every summer, scattered across her nose on her fair complexion. She tucked her blonde hair back behind her ear and sighed again. What a drive.

Still, it had been worth it. Ivy grabbed up her purse from the passenger seat and began rifling through it, looking for the appointment card the receptionist had given her. Dr. Patterson—that was his name. The man had been kind and calm and made her feel at ease, not like the last one. He had been a real creep. It was worth going an hour out of her way to avoid that.

Ivy hefted the straps of the purse onto the crook of her elbow and opened the car door, getting out with her keys and the slip of paper clutched in the other hand. She wanted to put it on the fridge as soon as she got in, so she wouldn't forget. The old doctor's card could go into the garbage. There was no way she was seeing him anymore, now that she had an alternative.

Ivy traipsed across the space between the barn and the house, listening to the silky sound of a light breeze running through the corn stalks. She couldn't feel it on her skin, but you could always hear the wind in the corn. It was a soundtrack that had marked her whole life, growing up on this farm with her family, something as familiar as the squawk of crows overhead and the lowing of the cows on the grazing pastures at the other side of the property.

She was halfway to the house when she heard something that made her pause and turn, looking into the stalks with a frown. Was that a whimper? It sounded almost like an animal. Maybe there was a fox in there, or a rabbit, or something else small that had been hurt. She thought of the family cat, Mr. Whipples, who lived in the barn and enjoyed a steady diet of mice and rats. He had been known to bring down the occasional larger animal, though, and he wasn't always fastidious about finishing them off.

Come to think of it, what if it was the cat himself?

"Mr. Whipples?" she called out softly, making the pss-pss-pss sound that always seemed to get his attention. There was no response. Not even another whimper.

Maybe she'd heard something different and just interpreted it wrong—a bird calling out on the other side of the field, for example. But it had sounded close enough.

Ivy was just deciding to turn back and go to the house, like she had originally intended, when her ears picked up on something else: rustling, not too far away again. Like something was moving through the stalks of the corn, turning the leaves aside as they went. It was out of time with the soft breeze, which seemed to have died now anyway. It was quiet enough that Ivy could hear, back on the other side of the house, one of the cows utter a low moan of frustration at the heat.

She took a few steps forward, right to the edge of the corn. Was something in there?

There was only one way that she was going to find out. Even if it was a wild animal, they sounded badly hurt. Most animals, even predators, wouldn't attack when they were injured. Especially not if the approaching thing was a human, so much bigger than them. It was probably safe. She told herself that, overriding the natural thrill of fear that went through her at the unknown.

Driven on by the fact that it could be Mr. Whipples, injured after taking on a wild scavenger too many, she pressed forward, pushing stalks gently out of the way with her hands to avoid doing any damage to the plant. She stepped carefully, watching the ground, her eyes flicking up to assess the way ahead and whether she could see the animal yet. It was eerily quiet now, the breeze gone completely. The only thing she could hear was the stalks slipping by on either side, and her own breathing, faster than it should have been.

Something moved ahead of her—a flash of dark through the gaps in the stalks.

Something way too tall to be a cat.

Too tall for any kind of animal. It was a person. There was someone in the corn with her.

Coming in further had been a mistake. Ivy froze for a second, then turned, knowing in her bones that something here was wrong. You didn't hide in the corn. Not for no reason. It wasn't going to be any of her family members—they knew better than to disturb the crops. Innocent tourists couldn't get out here on the private road. Whoever it was, they were lying in wait, and Ivy didn't want to stop to think about whether they had made the whimpering noise or something else had.

She broke into a run, pushing the corn stalks aside. They whipped at her face and arms, stinging her, and she dropped her purse on the ground to free up her hands and elbows for pushing. Why had she come so far into the field? Stupid! She saw the corn stalks thinning out ahead, the blue sky of the horizon visible now, almost close enough to make out her car and the pastures and the—

Something hit across the back of her head with a cracking noise, so loud and so sharp that she fell instantly. She had no idea what had happened until her brain caught up on processing to tell her that she was lying on the ground, surrounded by flattened and crushed corn stalks. Her first thought was that part of the harvest was ruined—only a small part, sure, but every plant mattered. Every plant was money to survive.

Ivy rolled over onto her back, hitting more stalks as she did so and trying not to crush them, aware of a strange groaning noise that she only slowly realized was coming from her own mouth. Someone was there—standing over her, framed by the corn, one of the stalks broken and drooping down in front of him. He was looking at her with an odd detachment, but it wasn't his face she was focused on. She was looking at his hands. One of them held a dark leather blackjack, and she was just beginning to understand the fact that she must have been hit with it.

The other hand held a machete.

"Please," Ivy managed to say, cutting off her own groan with some effort.

Then he stepped forward and raised the machete, and she could not gather enough thoughts in her brain to tell herself to scream.

CHAPTER TWELVE

Zoe paused just outside the room, looking around with an eyebrow raised in question. Shelley had grabbed hold of her arm from behind, prevented her from moving any further forward.

"Hey, listen," Shelley said, tucking herself comfortably against the wall. "I want you to try something."

Zoe frowned. She didn't like where this was going, already. "What do you mean?"

"I think you should take the lead on this one."

Zoe shook her head immediately. "That would be stupid. You are the better interrogator. We both know that."

Shelley smiled an easy smile, one that somehow simultaneously said thank you and you're too kind and other, similar sentiments. Zoe's smiles always only seemed to say I don't know how to do this or this is awkward, judging by both the reactions of others and what she saw in the mirror. How did Shelley do it?

"You've been watching me all this time. I know you have. And with the discussions we've had—you've learned a lot about technique, about how to use someone's emotions against them. I know you have."

Zoe felt her heartbeat rising inside her chest. She saw numbers rising all around Shelley—the distance between her eyes, the length of her nose, the diameter of the curve of the top of her head if it had formed a complete circle, the number of straight, white teeth that appeared when Shelley smiled and spoke again.

"Don't panic," she said. "You know this stuff. I'll be right next to you to help you out if you stumble. I really think you can do this. You can play him—use sympathy and emotion to manipulate him into telling the truth. He's a simple man. You can get him to confess."

66

"This is really important, Shelley," Zoe protested. "This isn't a training exercise. We are trying to take down a killer." The walls of the hallway were nine feet high, fifteen pieces of paper on the noticeboard over by the door, a shot fired at this distance from her handgun would penetrate the window and leave a hole of—

"I believe in you," Shelley said calmly. She reached out and laid a hand on Zoe's arm, a soothing influence. "Look beyond the numbers. Remember what we've worked on. The signs you can read. You're already great at this, you just don't know it yet."

Zoe swallowed, allowing Shelley's calm to touch her and transport her away, if only for a moment, to a tropical beach. A warm breeze stirred the upper branches of pine trees. She looked at Shelley again, and saw Shelley, not a series of calculations and measurements.

She took a deep breath and nodded once, firmly. She could do this. She pushed open the door before she could have second thoughts, and walked in with what she hoped was an air of confidence.

Zoe took a seat, then waited for Shelley to draw out her own chair and sit down beside her. The sheriff's interview room was small and cramped, with enough room for the four chairs and a small table, plus space to walk around the outside. It was low-tech: a camera positioned above the door in the corner was recording everything, but there was no double-sided glass or intercom system. They were alone.

Alone with Bob Taylor, who was slumped angrily in his seat, his wrists cuffed to a thick bar running under the table. There were red marks on his arms where he had struggled, and a slowly developing bruise on his right cheek. It had been deemed unlikely that he would need medical attention, thus freeing him up for their questions.

Zoe kept quiet for a moment, looking at Bob. Taking in the lines of his face, trying to see the emotions behind them instead of their length and depth.

Zoe hoped she was right. She took a breath, centering and calming herself. Bob Taylor was sullen and resentful of his treatment at the hands of the sheriff's boys. He didn't need a cop right now. He needed a friend.

"How does your face feel?" Zoe asked softly, trying to imbue the question with as much concern as she could.

Bob Taylor looked up in surprise and met her gaze. "It hurts. Funny, that."

Okay. He was angry, resorting to sarcasm as a defense mechanism. She hadn't gotten through to him yet. That was fine. Sometimes it took Shelley time to connect with the suspects. She had to put them at ease first. Right. Put him at ease.

"I'm sorry you were handled roughly," Zoe said, even though it was probably not the smartest thing to say—at least where the possibility of a lawyer was concerned. Thankfully, Bob Taylor had been angry enough when he came in to engage in a shouting match with the public defender, and had then waived his right to counsel with a number of curses directed toward the entire profession of lawyers. "Unfortunately, the sheriff's department got to you before we did."

Bob snorted, rattling his handcuffs against the table as he shifted. "You girls would have been a bit gentler, is it?"

Zoe ignored the barb and kept her facial expression smooth. "We just wanted to ask you a few questions, that's all. We might not even have needed to leave the property. All we need to do is clear a few things up and let you on your way."

"You didn't ask them to arrest me?" Bob said, half-incredulous. "I could have just talked to you there?"

"Of course," Zoe said, choosing her words carefully. "You look like a normal guy, Bob. Your boss says you're a good worker. The best installer in the county. It's not like you have anything to hide, right?"

"...Right," Bob agreed.

Zoe pretended that she had not noticed his hesitation, his uncertainty. Instead, she gave him a bright smile. She was sure it wasn't quite as effective as when Shelley did it—Shelley, with her bright blonde, feminine hair and her pink lipstick—but she tried all the same. "So, let's just show you a few photos and then we can chat about them really quick."

To her side, Shelley started pulling printed images out of the file she was holding. She waited, shielding the rest from Bob's view, as Zoe took the photograph of Michelle Young and put it in front of him.

"Do you know this woman?" Zoe asked.

Bob squinted at the picture. "She's been all over the news," he said.

"But before that," Zoe pressed, trying not to get impatient. "Did you recognize her, when you first saw her on the news?"

Bob pursed his lips and sniffed. "I did an installation for her, the day before."

"The day before what?"

"Before her picture was on the news."

Zoe cursed inwardly. She had wanted to catch him in a slip, to hear him say that he'd gone back the day after installing the machine to kill her. Instead, now he was looking at her with mounting suspicion, a frown creasing the already-deep furrows between his brows. She was losing him.

"All right," she said, smoothly. "Now, do you remember anything about the time you spent at her house? Did you see any other person? Anything unusual that stands out?"

"Nope." Bob shrugged. "Standard installation. Very clean place. Made me take off my shoes at the door. Still, in and out, nothing special."

"Do you remember her name?"

"Said Miss Young on the papers, so that's what I called her. In the news it said Michelle."

Zoe nodded, smiling as if he had done well already. "That's right. Now, do you remember how Miss Young was on that day? What was her attitude like?"

Bob frowned slightly, his eyes darting to the side and then up as he thought back. "She followed me around. I remember thinking she didn't trust me in her house. She hovered. Watched me while I worked and followed around after me with a bottle of disinfectant."

"That must have been off-putting for your work." Zoe laid the suggestion carefully, not wanting to arouse his suspicion again so quickly. It wouldn't be a good idea for him to think she was accusing him of anything. But to gauge his mood, whether he would have been angry with Michelle, angry enough to attack her, was crucial.

"A bit," Bob conceded. "Made me want to slow down and make sure I wasn't dirtying anything. But you can't do that, when you're on a job. You have to get it done as quick as possible and head back to depot for the next delivery."

"Now, did it seem to you that she was anxious about anything other than keeping the house clean?" Zoe asked.

Bob shrugged. "No. I thought she would give up watching after a while—a lot of them do. Once they see I'm good at my work. But this one, she kept over me the whole time. Barely said a word, just darting in with her spray to clean up every little surface whenever I gave her an opening."

Zoe hesitated. She seemed to have struck a vein—a topic that had caused enough irritation for Bob that he was willing to keep on talking about it, even without being prompted. Ideas were forming slowly in her mind, like flowers blossoming. "Did she allow you into any other part of the house beyond the installation site?" she asked.

Bob snorted, possibly at her use of the phrase "installation site," but he answered all the same. "She let me use her bathroom right before I left. Think it sent her into a shivering fit at the thought, but she could hardly say no."

There was something in his voice, a glee at the thought of upsetting the woman. Some kind of cruelty, like you might expect from a bully. But a bully was a far cry from a murderer. "Did you even need to use the bathroom?" Zoe asked. "Or did you just want to annoy her?"

Bob smirked. "I wanted to annoy the hag," he said. He was almost boastful. "It's hard to work like that, like I said. But I never went as far as to kill her. I wasn't that bothered by it."

Zoe was struck by the image of the bathroom as she had seen it during their inspection of the home. Everything spotless, except for one patch of wood on a shelf, stained a slightly different shade. As if something had sat there habitually for a long time, only to later be removed.

"You did do something, though, didn't you, Bob?" Zoe asked. She kept her tone light and casual, like this wasn't even really an accusation. "You took a little something from the bathroom, just to serve her right. To make the job more worth your while."

Bob looked uncomfortable, shifting in his seat and hesitating. He glanced to the side momentarily, as if looking for the lawyer that he had had the bad grace to dismiss. He was on his own in this room, and he knew it now.

"Just a...just a little thing," he said, glancing back and forth between Shelley and Zoe as if searching for a sign of how his confession was being received. "Just a little icon she had up there. A praying Mary. I thought it would be a little bit funny, you know? I was thinking of her panicking once she saw it was gone. It wasn't serious. I didn't—I mean, I didn't *kill* her."

Zoe held back a sigh of disappointment. She should have known by now to always trust her instincts. The feeling she had experienced of Bob not being their man had been right. He was guilty of a crime—just not the one they were investigating.

"You've developed a bit of a habit, haven't you?" she asked. "Taking little things."

"It's just like...a tip," Bob said, reaching now, desperate to explain away his behavior. "That's all. Just a tip for my work. For those that don't give one, or that make it hard work. That's all."

Zoe nodded, handing the image of Michelle Young back to Shelley. They didn't even need to go through the rest: she had seen enough. Bob wasn't their man, and he didn't know anything that could help them. He was too obsessed with his own string of petty crimes to have noticed a stalking killer.

"That's all for now," she told him, standing up. "A member of the sheriff's department will be in to continue your interview. I suggest you tell them everything. It might help you in court."

"Hey—hold on!" Bob exclaimed, obviously not happy at the prospect of being left with the very men who had beaten him. "No, wait a second!"

But Zoe was already leaving the room, Shelley in her wake.

A familiar gray head was approaching them down the corridor, clutching his hat in his hands. "Sheriff Hawthorne," Zoe said. "A pleasant coincidence. We are ready to hand Bob Taylor over to your team for further questioning. He is not our killer."

"I know," Hawthorne said gruffly, clearly trying to catch his breath as he paused in front of them. "That's what I was coming to tell you. He can't be the killer. We've just found another body—and it's fresh enough that it can't possibly have been Bob Taylor. He was already in custody."

Zoe reached into her pocket for the rental car keys. "Where?" she asked.

"Not far. I'll lead," the sheriff said, turning to race back along the corridor with Zoe and Shelley following close behind.

CHAPTER THIRTEEN

Zoe surveyed the horizon, just holding back a grimace. Though the corn
fields, the fences, and the farm's outbuildings blocked the view, she knew
what she would see beyond them. She knew this sky, knew the patchwork of
farmers' fields, the roads. She knew them well, because just over the ridge of the
next hill was a little town called Capten.

The town where she had grown up, and where the rest of her family still
lived, as far as she was aware.

"What is it?" Shelley asked softly. Zoe hadn't even heard her get out of the
car, but she was standing right beside her.

"I do not like it," she said.

"The murder, or this place?" Shelley asked. "I remember you saying you
grew up in a small town..."

Zoe met her eyes and realized that there was very little point in trying
to dissemble. Shelley had obviously read her like a book, just like she always
seemed to be able to. "A little town right over there," Zoe said, nodding her head
in the right direction.

Shelley glanced in through the open door of their car, studying the GPS.
"Capten."

"It's this way," Sheriff Hawthorne called out, interrupting their conversation. The way was obvious—his men had already cordoned off an area of the
waving corn stalks, in a circumference that also took in the ground in front
of them—but his comment was meant more, Zoe saw, as a means of hurrying
them up.

She didn't need another offer to get out of the awkwardness of talking
about her childhood. She strode forward, avoiding the area that the deputies
had marked off, where softer earth recorded a few footprints. They were female,

72

she saw instantly from the shape of the print, and belonged to a slim woman of five feet and six inches.

They had to be the steps of the victim. Zoe pressed on, walking carefully and examining the ground as she did so, marking only the footprints that were easily recognizable as the sheriff department's standard-issue heavy-duty foot-wear. No other signs littered the ground, and as she passed into a path that had been trampled through the corn, she entered a world of chaos.

The stalks seemed to be everywhere. Weaving around in the light breeze, they reached out to stroke or roughly brush her arms and legs, wanting to catch in her hair, trip up her feet. Zoe thought of a film she had seen as a child, the classic *Snow White*, with the branches of evil and haunted trees catching at the heroine's hair. Or was that some other fairytale character? She had never cared for them much, even back then.

The crime scene was obvious before she was fully upon it. Blood had splattered across stalks of corn for some distance, with their distinct pattern allowing it to run through gaps in their formation and splash some way away. Zoe held out a hand to warn Shelley—the tape did not extend this far in, no doubt because the deputies had some trouble getting it to weave through the crops.

The corn opened up suddenly into another flattened area, a glade that opened up in front of them like a parting of the seas. Trampled corn stalks made a soft bed of the floor, and on top of them lay their victim—all except her head, which, as by now Zoe would have predicted, was no longer attached to her shoulders.

"Stand still," she called out quickly, seeing with horror that the young deputies were tramping about in all directions, trying to take pictures of the scene. They all froze, a fact which Zoe enjoyed for a bare moment: it was nice to see her authority being respected.

But that was instantly replaced by a feeling of dread that perhaps crucial evidence had already been destroyed. The ground was even softer here amongst the stalks, and she saw a footprint that she did not recognize, half-overlaid by one of those standard-issue boots.

"There are footprints," she called out, her voice carrying to both the deputies, the sheriff, and Shelley behind her. "Nobody take another step until I've taken a look at them. This is the first sign of our killer."

There was begrudging silence as the sheriff and his men stood still. The younger ones shifted for a moment, until a look from Hawthorne had them freezing again, guilty looks plastered across their faces. They clearly knew when they were being reprimanded.

Zoe ignored them, ignored all of the rest of it, and put the soft sighing of the wind through the corn stalks out of her mind. It could almost sound like a voice if you were paying too much attention, and she could not be distracted now. She moved forward carefully, bending low to the ground, taking one step at a time. She examined the ground ahead for footprints of any kind, not just to avoid stepping over them but also to get an idea of where the killer had gone.

The marks emerged from under the clumsy deputy's prints about fifty yards from the body, peeling away through the corn. The footprints were almost all incomplete—it was difficult to walk here without stepping on the corn itself—but then they hit a broader opening, a lane designed for the farmer's access, and moved with more confidence.

Zoe crouched as low as she could, and let her eyes read the numbers right off the ground itself. They were looking for a male, almost certainly now, because he wore men's boots and he was six feet tall. He weighed about a hundred and sixty pounds, and he walked with the slow confidence of a man who was sure of not getting caught. How could he have been so sure? According to the sheriff, this woman's body had been discovered by her family within fifteen minutes, after they noticed her car in the yard but no one in it.

He had an arrogance about him, she realized. All this time they had thought he was unafraid, that he planned things out so well he had no fear of getting caught. But in this case there had been nothing to stop him from being found in the act. If one of her family had looked out of the window sooner, he might have even been interrupted. It wasn't the confidence of planning: it was some supreme belief in his own abilities, the cockiness of a superiority complex.

He was mocking them, all of them, with every body he took.

Zoe retraced her steps, carefully, making sure to step exactly back in her own prints. "He went in that direction," she called out, pointing for the benefit of the deputies. "There's a trail through the corn, then you hit a broader path and he carries on. You should follow his footprints. Record them as you go. Don't step on them."

They had enough sense, at least, to look guilty as they sloped off amongst the corn. An eerie rustling accompanied their progress. If Sheriff Hawthorne took umbrage at Zoe giving orders to his own men, he said nothing.

With the deputies rustling across the field behind them, and only the three of them left with the body, the atmosphere was even more eerie. "Anything unusual?" Zoe asked, referring to the time Shelley had already had to examine the victim and the scene.

"Same story," Shelley said. "She was probably lured out here by some noise, given that her tracks lead right from her car. It looks as though she was knocked to the ground, here, and flattened these stalks when she tried to roll away. Then he took her head."

The grim statement was still no match for the reality of it. The headless corpse lay prostate on the ground, the soil and the trampled stalks and leaves of corn under it stained a sickly red. The gore was splattered across the stalks all around it, except in one place: the spot from where the killer's footprints led back.

If he was still around, he would be easy to spot. The blood would have splashed over him, littering his clothes with tell-tale signs. Even so, Zoe couldn't even bring herself to hope that it would be that easy. Whoever he was, he was smart enough to be long gone by now.

"I agree with that assessment," Zoe said. It was true: the body could tell her nothing else that Shelley had not already pointed out. Even if she couldn't see the numbers, she was getting good at reading the signs. Noticing correlation. The way that this crime scene held just the same clues as the others.

"What about the prints?" Shelley asked. The sheriff was still nearby, staring grimly down at the body with his hands on his hips, and Zoe didn't want to give too much away. Not until he was no longer listening.

"Looks like an able-bodied male, to me," Zoe said. She could share the precise calculations for weight and height later, and then they could work on putting together evidence which explained these conclusions for those who couldn't see what she could. "He did not run—just walked, calmly, as if nothing was wrong in the world. I noted a trail of blood drips alongside his steps, most likely from the machete and the head. The prints led towards the back of the fields. I wouldn't be surprised if the deputies traced them to some small road back there, one with fresh indentations from a vehicle parked at the side of it for a while."

"He hid his presence well," Sheriff Hawthorne spoke up at last. "The family didn't notice a thing until it was too late. I've got Miranda sitting with them for now. We could go speak to them."

His deference was both refreshing and a little concerning. There was something in the pallor of his skin under that gray hair that worried Zoe. He must never have dealt with anything like this before, not out here where the living was often so slow you wouldn't see a really serious case for months. Now a string of gruesome beheadings of young women, all right on his doorstep. Zoe only hoped he wasn't about to give up on the investigation or start putting roadblocks in their way. So long as he was cooperative, nothing else mattered.

"This is bold, so close to the house," Shelley said, as they pushed their way back through the rustling stalks.

Zoe winced as the edge of one of the leaves drew a faint slash across her forearm, leaving a raised red mark. "It feels like he's getting more confident as time goes on. He never quite takes the risk of killing in front of witnesses, but he takes risks all the same."

"It's a thrill." Shelley was slightly breathless as they pushed out of the last of the stalks and into open space again. "He gets a thrill out of taking their lives, and each time the stakes get higher, that adrenaline rush is bigger. He'll only continue to be bolder, more provocative. That thrill has to get bigger and bigger every time, or he won't be satisfied."

It was textbook stuff—the kind of thing they taught you at the Academy in Quantico. Escalation, rapidity, all the hallmark traits of a serial killer on a destructive cycle. Eventually their hubris would get them caught, though you really aimed to stop them from killing before it became inevitable. Zoe knew all of this information, all of the data about human behavior, but she often still needed Shelley to translate it for her and remind her that it had a human face.

There was another set of faces they would have to be confronted with, however, before they could go back to their base at the sheriff's station and put the data to good use. Zoe's least favorite part of any investigation: the grieving family.

"Marle," Sheriff Hawthorne said at the door to the cheery, red-brick farmhouse, taking off his hat respectfully as he stepped inside and greeted an older woman sitting in a cluttered living area. As Zoe filed in after him, she took in literally hundreds of tchotchkes scattered around every visible surface of the room, surrounding the female deputy and an older couple. Sitting just apart from them on a low armchair was a younger woman, with dark hair and generous sweepings of mascara and kohl now smudged helplessly around her eyes. Even without being introduced, Zoe could see the family resemblance: parents and daughter.

"This is Special Agents Zoe Prime and Shelley Rose, from the FBI," Hawthorne was saying gently, as he sunk down onto an embroidered stool opposite the family. "They're here to get to the bottom of whoever is doing this."

"They'll find who did this to our Ivy?" the older woman, who Hawthorne had addressed as Marle, half-sobbed.

"We hope so. Agents, let me introduce you to Marlene and Danny Griffiths. This is their daughter, Scarlet. Ivy's younger sister."

Ivy Griffiths. Zoe realized with a start that she had not even asked for the victim's name until now. She was getting too deep into this one, starting to see the victims only as numbers and data rather than real people. She had to bring herself back down, keep trying to see things the way that Shelley saw them. Glancing to her side as she edged into the room, seeing nowhere to sit and hovering awkwardly behind Hawthorne, she noticed Shelley's eyes gleaming with bright compassion.

"We appreciate that this is a very difficult time for you all, and we're sorry for your loss," Shelley said warmly, lifting the eyes of the family to her. "But if we can ask you a few questions now and get it all over with, we might be able to find a crucial lead which helps us crack this case."

The father seemed numb to whatever was going on around him, simply staring ahead with a blank pallor. Marlene and Scarlet, however, nodded their assent, in varying degrees of tearfulness.

"All right." Shelley moved a half-step forward. She kept her shoulders relaxed, her hands clasped lightly in front of her. A non-threatening pose that exuded calm. Zoe, lagging that half step behind, felt it fill the room as she watched. "Let's start with what you saw or heard before you realized what had happened."

"Nothing," Marlene said, shaking her head, distress written plain across her face. "I didn't hear anything. I didn't even know Ivy was home."

"I heard her car pull in," Scarlet said. Her voice was quieter than her mother's, more subdued. "I didn't think anything of it. It's a familiar sound. When she didn't come in right away I thought she must be with the cows or something."

"Did you hear anything from the cows?" Zoe cut in, trying to keep her voice as measured and light as Shelley's was. "Anything that might have made you think someone was over there?"

Scarlet shook her head. "I just assumed. It was about fifteen minutes before I looked out and realized she still hadn't come in. Then I—I thought I'd better look, and I saw the corn..."

She fell silent. Zoe had seen the way the corn looked from the outside, a broken horizon, jagged shapes where there should have been a smooth line. A broken pattern. Obvious enough to any farmer who knew the state of their crop.

"What about you, Danny?" Shelley pressed gently, directing a quiet voice toward the patriarch. He stirred vaguely, then shook his head, a fast and sharp gesture at odds with his dreamlike state.

Zoe shifted restlessly. There were no answers here. A house full of people who hadn't even noticed a thing. Maybe arrogance wasn't really arrogance when you were right about how good you were.

"Where was Ivy before she came home?" Shelley asked. "Does she work outside of the farm?"

"No, we all help out here," Marlene said. Her hands, folded on her lap, were creased and darkened from long hours of manual work in the sun, Zoe noted. "She was out at a doctor's appointment, I think."

"Are you aware of your daughter knowing someone named Michelle Young?" Shelley asked, looking across a row of blank faces for confirmation. "Lorna Troye? No?"

"Do you have any outside help?" Zoe asked, hitting on an idea. "Farmhands, or the like?"

Marlene shook her head, but to Zoe's surprise, it was Danny who answered. "Not since last harvest season. Couldn't afford them. Last year's yield was low. Ivy helped us this year. Took on a lot more work. She was a good gir—" His voice broke, splintering away abruptly into nothingness, and his wife grabbed hold of his knee and squeezed it.

Zoe knew private grief when she saw it. It was a thing that had always been inaccessible to her, a closed-off garden, an island surrounded by deep waters.

She couldn't understand it, had never been through it, had no points of reference to reach them with. There was nothing she could do here.

Shelley seemed to feel the same way, or at least to feel that the time for questions was over. "Thank you," she said. "You've been very helpful. I'm going to leave my card on the table here—I want you to get in touch with me if you think of anything, absolutely anything, that might help. No matter how small."

They left behind a broken shell of a family, with an empty space that would never be filled again. Zoe stalked back to the car in silence, then sat inside with a sigh of frustration.

"What now?" Shelley asked. "We don't exactly have many leads."

"We wait for the sheriff's boys to report back on the tracks I sent them following," Zoe said. She squinted up at the sky, by now already darkening. "And we go and find a room for the night."

CHAPTER FOURTEEN

Zoe stood just outside the motel's office, looking up at the sky. It was clear enough, even here, that she could see the stars, glittering against pure darkness. It had been a long time since she lived anywhere but a major city. Being in this open space, with only the two stories of the motel blocking out the view behind her, felt strange. Almost surreal.

Maybe that wasn't it at all, because she had taken on plenty of cases that were in out-of-the-way corners of the country. Some of them had been quick jobs that took barely any time to solve, and others required more in-depth concentration, more nights spent in motels like this one. No, maybe it was the fact that she was so close to the place where she had grown up. Her formative years had been under this sky, and even though it might theoretically have been the same sky that one could see from anywhere in the world, there was something about it that just kept on sending a shiver down her spine.

"Come on," Shelley said, leaving the motel office with a weary look. Her shoulders were slumped, echoing Zoe's own posture: the exhaustion of a long day after a very short night, coupled with utter frustration at the lack of leads they had.

The sheriff had called them as they drove over to the motel they'd found online, letting them know that his deputies had followed the footprints back to a local by-road, as she had suspected. But there was no mark on the soil there to suggest a parked car, and thus no tire tracks they could use to get an imprint. He had been clever. Walked down the road from further away, perhaps, or left the car running on the tarmac so as to not leave any sign.

Not clever enough to avoid leaving footprints, though. Zoe took some small comfort in that.

They dragged their overnight bags from the trunk of the car and into their motel rooms, going through the usual ritual of testing the fittings, bouncing a hand on the bed to assess the quality of the mattress, pulling a face at the scratchiness of the sheets. Zoe poked her head into the bathroom and noted a couple of missing tiles revealing bare walls. It reminded her in a funny way of her uncle, a man she hadn't seen in over fifteen years, and the broken tile down near the toilet in his house where he had accidentally kicked it once while drunk.

Zoe passed a hand over her eyes. There were too many ghosts in this town. The biggest of them all was the elephant in the room, the one she dared not turn and address. If she did, she would have to face a whole can of memories opened up like worms, and there wasn't room for that in a murder investigation.

Shelley opened her door without knocking and sat down on the edge of Zoe's bed, her nails scrabbling against wood as she dug out a few takeout menus from the drawer beside it. "We should get some dinner," she said. "Do you want to go out, or get something delivered?"

The thought of going out to a diner and running into someone she used to know made Zoe shudder. "Delivery would be best," she said, though truth be told, she was barely even hungry.

She sat down on the other side of the bed and smoothed her hand across the threadbare covers. They bore a rustic pattern, quite old-fashioned, but not out of place here in this rural settlement. Not unlike, actually, the sheets her mother had kept for the spare room in case of guests—

Ah. And there it was.

The spare room. Zoe had hated it mercilessly. When it was prim and undisturbed, her mother would punish her liberally, making her kneel and pray, forcing her to stop seeing the numbers—or, in fact, to stop talking about them, because she had only recently learned any modicum of control. Then when guests came they had to be on their best behavior, which was at least a relief but also a minefield; and when the guests were gone, Zoe knew, whatever mindless infractions she had committed would be meted out on her over and over again until her mother was satisfied.

Not that she was ever satisfied.

"What do you think, Zoe?"

Zoe looked up and saw that Shelley was watching her with an eyebrow raised, a slight aura of impatience. "Sorry, what?"

"You weren't listening? I just read out all of the options." Shelley sighed. "What's going on with you today? Is it being this close to home?"

Zoe had already made her decision. It had just taken her this long to accept that. She stood, getting her coat from the back of the chair where she had draped it, and dropped her cell phone into the pocket. "I'm going out," she said. "Have dinner without me. I'll eat while I'm out."

"Are you sure? Z?"

But Zoe was already leaving, throwing the motel room door shut behind her as she descended into the night and toward the rental car.

Uncle Mike's house was the same as she remembered it. It was a little more weather-worn, maybe, and there were signs of a fresh paint job that had been done long enough ago to be peeling already. The car in the drive was a newer model. Still, it was recognizable, in that way that houses have of staying the same under the same ownership. Five familiar windows looked out at her like eyes, around the mouth of a door of the same width and diameter as the one in her memory.

It had crossed Zoe's mind that Uncle Mike might have moved away. He and Aunt Julie had been very settled in Capten, as far as she remembered, but that didn't necessarily mean the intervening fifteen years hadn't changed that. But somehow, standing here and looking up at the house, she knew they were still here.

This had been a poor idea. What was she thinking, going to see a family she had been estranged from for so long? It was a fishing expedition, really: to ask about her mother, because even if she never wanted to see her again, there was still curiosity there. Somewhere, buried down deep, she still cared at least a little bit about whether her mother was doing well.

No; it wasn't worth it. She shouldn't be here. Zoe turned and opened the door of her car—only to hear another door opening close by.

"Zoe? That's you, isn't it?"

Zoe turned again, looking up at her Uncle Mike, framed by yellow light spilling out from his open doorway. He was older than she had expected. Her memories had been distorted by the passage of time, and maybe that same time had not been kind to Mike. His hair was almost all gone, the tufts that remained thin and gray, and he had developed a paunch that stuck out in front of him like a ball. She wondered if he had not lost an inch in height.

"It is me," she said, drawing in a deep breath of the cool night air. She had been ready to make her escape, but it seemed that that was no longer an option.

"What are you doing, standing outside in the heat?" Mike asked, though Zoe couldn't help feel it was a mechanical question, one of rote rather than of feeling. "Come on inside."

As Zoe approached and stepped over the threshold, Mike disappeared in front of her down the thin hallway she remembered; dimly, somewhere in the family room, she heard him saying, "It *is* her, Jules. I told you."

Zoe followed him, automatically kicking her shoes off by the rack full of others and pulling the door closed behind her. She padded in her socks through to the cramped family room, full of sagging couches and armchairs that had seen better days. Aunt Julie was there, also a victim of middle-aged spread— at least thirty pounds since the last visit—and with graying hair. Under two expectant pairs of eyes, Zoe chose the seat that appeared to have the least number of stains on it.

"It's been a long while since you were in these parts," Aunt Julie said. "What, twenty years?"

"Fifteen," Zoe corrected her. She had been sixteen years old when she emancipated herself from her mother and left. She hadn't ever intended to look back. The uncomfortable sensation of being back here, a place that ostensibly had no bad memories but was linked to so many others, made her feel like the walls were crushing in on her. She could barely breathe, let alone figure out how she was supposed to act.

"Fifteen years, and not even a call," Aunt Julie tutted. "Your mama always did say you were ungrateful."

Zoe's blood ran cold. If she had expected a warm welcome, this was certainly not it. She didn't even know what she had expected, come to think of it, but this was no happy reunion. And something about that past tense, too...

"I have been making my way in the world," she said, by way of an excuse, she supposed, although it didn't sound strong to even her own ears. She shifted the front of her jacket slightly, letting it fall open to show the badge at her hip. "I am an FBI agent."

"You one of those FBI working the killings that happened here?" Aunt Julie asked. When Zoe nodded, she tsked in return, shifting one weighty hip against her seat. "Took a killing to bring you back here. Huh. Some family visit."

"Kept you busy for fifteen years, bein' FBI, did it?" Uncle Mike grunted from his battered armchair. He looked as though he were sinking into the fabric, like it might just end up swallowing him whole. Zoe was about to agree, until she realized the statement was a judgmental one, not one of sympathy.

She looked at the floor for a moment, twining her hands together, trying to think of what to say. "I put everything into my work," she said. Then, realizing that it made her sound like a friendless old maid who had wasted her life, she added: "And I am seeing someone."

That had not improved things; she felt it as her words faded into the air. Everything she said seemed to be the wrong thing. Julie and Mike were staring at her from under furrowed brows, their eyes beetle-black and hard, examining her for any sign of defect. She was sure that they saw many.

"It's a shame you couldn't find your way back here before your mama died," Julie sighed. "Leaving her all alone at the end like that."

A jolt ran through Zoe's heart, a squeeze of pain that was entirely unexpected. Her mother was dead?

"When?" she gasped out, the only thing that came to her mind. If she had been more in control she might have tried to appear unaffected and unsurprised, then looked into the death records herself. She didn't have that presence, not in the moment.

"A few years back." Julie shook her head and took a sip of some kind of brown liquid from a cheap, picnic-style glass, the happy design on the outside chipping off. "No one even knew how to reach you. She would have been mortified to know you didn't even come to her funeral."

"I did not know." Zoe's voice came out as a whisper, and she tried to gather more strength. "No one called."

"You never called anyone here, honey," Julie told her, the "honey" coming out like a sneer instead of a term of endearment. "How was we supposed to know where to get you?"

"The phonebook," Zoe said, before she could stop herself. "Social media."

"Don't get smart with us," Uncle Mike grunted. "You wasn't here, and that's the long and short of it. Running off like that after your mama spent so much time raising you. Without a backward glance. Some gratitude, hm!"

Zoe wet her lips, trying to think her way through this. Everything they were saying crowded in on her, like waves one after the other, threatening to drown her. None of them had seen what it was like for her, just a child, forced to believe that she was a product of the devil. Persecuted for an ability she had no control over.

She thought about the spare room in her childhood home. How whenever someone was in it, the punishments stopped. Walking on eggshells and knowing she would mess up anyway. Trying not to let on that she was different. Dreading the day the guests left and she would kneel all night on the cold floor, whispering her prayers over and over until her mouth was dry and her lips cracked and bleeding.

"How did it happen?" she asked, her voice barely a whisper. She could not see Julie and Mike, not anymore. She was looking down at their carpet, an interlocking woven pattern formed into heraldry and foliage, an imitation of a historic pattern. She knew that carpet. She remembered there were sixteen deer between the sides of the room, at least that you could see. Under the furniture, she had once calculated, there were seven more.

"Cancer," Aunt Julie pronounced with a sigh. "Got her quick. Wasn't long in the hospital. Shock to us all."

"Lot of cancer round these parts," Uncle Mike added. "Cousin John, too."

Zoe wasn't sure she had ever met a cousin John. Perhaps Mike meant his own cousin. The information washed over her, one thing after another, so quick and close that it was difficult to filter out what was important and what was useless.

"And your Aunt Debbie got married again," Aunt Julie said. "Y-e-e-e-p, you missed that one too."

"That was a good wedding," Uncle Mike noted.

Zoe felt a kind of rushing in her head, a sensation of everything coming over her at once. It was all too much. Being back here had been the first thing, but hearing that her mother had died, the judgment, the news she didn't need or care about—it was too much. She had to get out.

"Of course it was a good wedding," Aunt Julie tsked again. "You acting like we can't put on a good wedding. Debbie knows what she's about. Not going to let miss stuck-up city life here think we can't do a good wedding out here in the country like anyone can."

"I do not think that," Zoe tried to say, hoping that somehow it would take the heat off her.

"Well, why didn't you come to the wedding?" Uncle Mike asked. "If you ain't too good for us, you would've been here."

How to put it into words? The years of abuse, of psychological torture, of being made to feel like she was evil and sinful. The years it had taken, afterwards, to have any kind of belief in herself. The kind of damage that might have been done if she had ever come back, especially before she had met Dr. Applewhite, or before she had become an FBI agent, or before she had started working with Shelley.

In the end, she didn't have an excuse, not one she was willing to say out loud. She couldn't stay here anymore, with the faded and smoke-stained wallpaper closing in on her, with their judgmental eyes burning holes in her skin. The numbers were getting uncontrollable, and there was so much here to count: the clutter, the furniture crowded in, the faded and lumpy bodies of her relatives. She couldn't think of what people normally said to exit these situations politely. She couldn't remember the right words.

"Then Bob, remember, Janie's boy," Uncle Mike said, plowing right over her lack of a response. "You missed all that noise, too."

"Oh, Mike, really," Aunt Julie barked, shaking her head. "You're gonna tell her about that one? She don't need to know about no jailbreaking hotshot, making us sound like the scum of the earth over here. What about Janie's girl—what's her name . . ."

"Sandy," Uncle Mike said.

"No, not Sandy—Sandra—she was a good girl. Got herself a good job over the state border now. Four kids too. Unlike some."

Zoe got up with a rush, almost knocking over a stack of old magazines by the side of the chair. "I should go," she said, barely even hearing her own words. From somewhere the bolt of inspiration had come to her. "It is late."

"Just about as expected," Uncle Mike said, smacking his lips together loudly. "Got something more important than us to deal with, I bet."

Zoe hesitated in the hallway, looking back into the family room. Neither of them had shifted from their chairs to see her out. She felt like she might rage and yell at them, or break down in tears, or beg them to look at her, really look at her. Instead she lifted her chin, fingering the car keys in her pocket. "I have a serial killer to catch," she said, shortly, and strode out of the house without listening for a response.

CHAPTER FIFTEEN

Shelley unlocked her motel door and paused before walking in, glancing through the gap in the curtains of the room next door: no Zoe. It had been partially expected. After all, Zoe had said she was going out somewhere and would be eating on her own, so she might well be out all night. There was no sense waiting up for her—though Shelley knew at least part of her would be finely tuned, listening, until she heard that door open and close through the wall.

She pushed her way into her room, and was just turning to close the door behind her when she recognized the rental car pulling up into the parking lot. She'd had to take a taxi to a local diner, and she had half a mind to tell Zoe off for taking the car without asking, although in her heart she knew she wasn't really mad. Something was off with her partner, had been all day, and Shelley didn't want to push her too hard.

She waited in her doorway, hesitating, then dropped her bag on the floor and joined Zoe as she went into her own room. Without asking, she followed her, putting down a small plastic bag on the desk.

"What is that?" Zoe asked, nodding her head toward the bag. Shelley noticed that her formality was back and held back a wince. Something had happened, and whatever it was, it wasn't good.

"I got leftovers," Shelley said. "I asked them to pack it up for me. Just in case you didn't get a chance to eat anything."

Zoe was busy, hanging up her jacket, unpacking things from her bag, setting the motel room key carefully at a precise angle on the dresser. "I am not hungry," she said.

"Thank you for being so thoughtful, Shelley," Shelley muttered under her breath. She shook her head; Zoe either hadn't heard the comment or was pretending not to have. Sometimes, the similarities between being partnered with Zoe and looking after her four-year-old daughter were startling. Louder, she tried again. "You should at least eat something. So you can keep your strength up for the case, if nothing else."

"Maybe." Zoe refused to commit. She was hanging clothes up, neat suits and shirts that had been crumpled up in her overnight bag.

"Z…" Shelley sighed, knowing the best approach was head-on where Zoe was concerned. "What happened? Where did you go?"

"Nothing happened," Zoe said, yanking one of her jackets straight on the hanger with a sharp movement. "I am tired. We should get some sleep."

Shelley took a breath. Whatever it was, it was bad—she knew that much. It was written all over Zoe. And if it was bad enough that she didn't want to talk about it, that usually meant it was something that absolutely needed talking about.

This called for the big guns. Shelley didn't really like using her techniques on friends—there was something traitorous about it—but she needed to get to the bottom of this. If she didn't, it might fester away, and Zoe had made such good progress over the past few months. She didn't want her friend to throw all of that away.

The Reid technique was one of her favorites, and it applied here: it was clear that something was wrong. Getting it out of Zoe was the point, but there was no chance she would be able to deny it. Not convincingly. Shelley sat down at the chair by the room's desk, swiveling it around to face Zoe, and began the first step: *Tell the suspect you know they did it because of the evidence presented, and give them a chance to explain.*

"Something happened tonight," Shelley said. "I can tell by the way you are. I know something happened to you. Why don't you tell me what's got you so upset?"

Zoe pursed her lips together, refolding a set of pajamas despite the fact she had indicated that she wanted to sleep. "I am not upset."

The lie was an obvious one. Shelley moved on. *Shift the blame away from the suspect to another person or set of circumstances; justify or excuse the crime.* "Someone must have done or said something," Shelley said. "You were coping all right with being here. Someone must have set this off, hmm? Who was it?"

Zoe gritted her teeth. "I told you, I am fine."

Minimize the frequency of suspect denials. "I don't believe that. You don't have to pretend with me, Z. I can tell."

"It does not matter."

"Of course it matters, Z," Shelley told her soothingly. *Reinforce sincerity.* "I care about you. Come on. Just tell me what's bothering you. Maybe I can help."

Zoe shot her a sharp look, and stopped taking her toiletries out of her bag. She set her toothbrush, wrapped in a separate plastic bag, down on the bed, and continued to stare right at Shelley, her brows knitting together. "You are using a technique on me."

Oh dear. "No, Z, I just want to get to the bottom of what's going on. I know someone has upset you."

"Yes, you are. What was it?" Zoe's eyes sharpened with clarity, her fingers snapping together. "Reid. You were using Reid on me."

If anything, Shelley was startled that Zoe had recognized it. Since she had, maybe trying to deny it was not the best option. "I'm just trying to get you to open up. You need to talk about things."

"No, I do not." Zoe's voice was firm and rough, like a thunderclap. "I am not a suspect. You cannot interrogate me."

"I know that, of course, but—"

"I am not one of your subjects. I thought we were becoming friends."

Zoe's words cut Shelley to the core. She was right, of course. It wasn't good behavior to use police interrogation techniques on your friends. Shelley knew that, but she was good at it—it was the whole basis of her reputation within the Bureau. It was hard not to rely on those techniques, and it was also hard not to fall back on them when someone didn't want to open up. What else was she supposed to do? Just let Zoe wallow in her feelings, alone and unheard, until she reached a breaking point?

"We are friends," Shelley said quietly. "That's why I'm concerned about you."

Zoe strode toward her across the room, taking her none too gently by the arm and pulling her up out of the chair. "I do not need your kind of concern," she snapped. She frog-marched Shelley to the door, only letting her go once she was outside.

As the door slammed in her face, Shelley reflected that she probably deserved it. Now she knew what it felt like to be treated like a suspect—and, she had to admit, it wasn't pleasant at all.

✤   ✤   ✤

Zoe paced back and forth restlessly, unable to stay still. There were so many things moving around in her head: Uncle Mike and Aunt Julie with their coldness, the fact of her mother's death, Shelley's condescension, the fact that she cared enough to try, the leftover food, the hunger that clawed at her belly but refused to be satisfied.

She went to the desk and opened the bag, drawing out a small paper box that had been carefully folded shut. In it was a full sandwich, cut in half to fit inside the box—thick white bread, lettuce, bacon, juicy slices of tomato. They weren't leftovers. Shelley had bought her a meal.

Zoe took a bite, found it to be surprisingly good. She closed her eyes as the mouthful slid down her throat, feeling the painful clench of her empty stomach crying out for more. She devoured the rest of the sandwich quickly, keeping her eyes closed except to fish out the second half. There was a storm building right between her eyes, and if she just kept them closed, the water couldn't leak.

With the sandwich gone, she felt better—at least, fuller. Her stomach was no longer raging and pinching in, and that was an improvement. But the rest was still there, swirling around, a storm cloud gathering force and darkness.

There was only one person in this whole town—this whole state—who cared enough to help her weather that storm. She was only being stupid, pushing her away. Zoe could see that now. Before she could change her mind, she walked outside and knocked on her neighbor's door, hoping that she hadn't already gone to sleep.

The door opened after just a moment's pause, revealing Shelley, dressed in a floral nightgown and with her hair, for once, hanging down around her shoulders.

"I'm sorry," Zoe said, quickly, before Shelley had the chance to open her mouth. It was important that she get that bit out, before anything else. "I was being unfair. I am upset, and I was trying to take it out on you."

"I know." Shelley's face and voice were soft, unaccusatory. "I shouldn't have tried to get it out of you like that. I'm sorry, too."

Zoe's lips quirked into an imitation of a smile. "You don't need to apologize," she said. "Can I come in?"

Shelley stepped aside, letting her in before closing the door behind her. They both sat down on the lone bed, a double with enough space that they could sit side-by-side, propped up against the thin pillows.

Shelley waited patiently, not saying a word. Zoe understood that it was her place, now, to open up, if she wanted to. Somehow, she found that she did.

"I went to visit family," she began, her voice holding steady. Detached. It was the only way she could look at these things, even within her own mind. "My aunt and uncle. They were not happy to see me."

"Why not?" Shelley asked. If there was judgment in her voice, it was only toward those who had hurt Zoe. She could understand that now, after enough time as Shelley's partner. She was a protective mother bear, always fiercely loyal to those she cared for.

"Because they think I abandoned my family when I left. That I just walked out with no reason and never looked back."

"That's not true," Shelley said. It was a statement, rather than a question.

"No. They just never knew what was really going on at home. They only saw the perfect image my mother wanted them to see."

There was a small chasm of silence, growing deeper by the second, until Shelley said, "What was really going on?"

Grateful for the cue, Zoe continued. "I have always had the numbers. Even when I was a little girl. Back then, I didn't realize that what I could do was different. I thought everyone could see them. Naturally, my mother was the first person to find out what I could do. What I could see." She cleared her throat, studying the back of her own hand, idly counting and measuring veins and tendons. "She thought I was possessed by the devil. Or that I had devil's blood in my veins. I was not ever really clear on that. She tended to give mixed messages when she was screaming at me."

Almost reflexively, Shelley's hand moved over and gripped one of Zoe's, squeezing it tightly. It was only when she eased off a touch that Zoe continued.

"She made me pray. For hours—even all night, sometimes. She would force me to kneel on the floor and pray that God would take the evil out of me. She forbade me from using the numbers or letting on to anyone else that I could see them, but it would always come out one way or another. At school, at home. I was an outcast. No friends. They all thought I was a freak. And at home, I was the devil child. She wanted me to stop being what I was. I couldn't. Not even if she beat all the skin off my bones, I wouldn't have been able to. Gradually I learned to hide it, to try to be normal. But I was never quite normal enough for her."

Zoe blinked, finding to her surprise that her eyelashes were wet. "Things came to a head over and over again. She would destroy things that I liked, curse and scream at me, anything to try to humiliate or hurt me. In front of others, we had to be the perfect apple pie family, no arguments, no slip-ups. But I always managed to make some kind of mistake. And then she would look at me and I—I just knew what was waiting as soon as we were alone. It went on for so long I ended up believing her. But no amount of prayer would make me better. In the end, when I was a teenager, I grew to realize that I could not change. And if I could not change, then I also could not stay. I got myself legally emancipated and left. I never looked back."

"You haven't spoken to your mother since?" Shelley asked. She had taken all of the rest of it in stride, and while her voice was heavy with pity, at least she wasn't pushing Zoe away. She wasn't disgusted by her. That fear that Zoe had held onto all of her life, that those who knew her secret would despise her, was chipping away, flaking to the floor, with every kind gesture Shelley showed her.

"No," Zoe said. "And I didn't even know. Uncle Mike and Aunt Julie just told me. She...she died a few years ago."

Shelley gasped, squeezing Zoe's hand harder; a moment later she let go entirely and threw her arms around Zoe, pulling her close. Zoe stiffened momentarily, at first simply enduring the embrace. Then she relaxed, and realized that she needed it. A sob racked through her body, the sound seeming to come from somewhere else, someone else. Like a dam had been released or a tap turned on, tears began to stream down her face, their rhythm out of time with the staccato breaths that she couldn't seem to get control of.

It was like all the emotion of the years of her life that she had kept buried deep inside suddenly came to the surface. She had never let it out or given it voice before, certainly not like this.

There was no sadness inside of her for the loss of her mother. It was not that she was gone—that, if anything, was something of a relief. But as she cried, her body racked with convulsive breaths and her face unfamiliarly wet, she knew that she was crying for herself: the fact that she had never really had a mother at all.

"I didn't know it was that bad," Shelley said, stroking her back carefully. "I knew you had some pain in your past by the way you were around small towns, but I could never imagine . . ."

Perhaps because she rarely cried, Zoe could not stop for a long time. When she was finally empty, her eyes dry and stinging, there was an emptiness inside her—but not a cold void; rather, a place that had once been filled with fear and misery and was now simply a hole. It was welcome. And, as she left to go into her own room, Zoe couldn't help but reflect that now maybe, at last, she could fill it with something else—something that came from those like Shelley who supported her instead.

CHAPTER SIXTEEN

*Z*oe looked down at her own small body, outfitted in a faded "Jesus Saves" T-shirt and floral-patterned leggings, both picked out by her mother. What was she supposed to do? Wasn't there something that was required of her?

She couldn't quite grasp what it was, but she knew two things: first, that it had something to do with her T-shirt, and second, that if she didn't do it, she would be in a lot of trouble. Her mother was probably coming even now. She had to do something, quickly, or her mother would be mad at her again.

But what was it?

"Are you ready, darling?"

The voice that called out to her instantly filled her with a sense of calm and belonging. Ah, her mother was here! That was right—there was no reason to be afraid. Her mother was here, and everything was all right.

"I think so," she replied, her voice coming out sweet and higher-pitched than she expected. "Do you need me to bring anything?"

"Just yourself. Come here, let me look at you." Zoe turned to see her mother there in the doorway, offering her a gentle smile under the bob of her hair. "Yes, you look perfect. We're going to have so much fun today."

Dr. Applewhite held out her hand, and Zoe rushed forward to take it. "Where are we going?"

"To your favorite place in the whole wide world, of course," Dr. Applewhite laughed. "Where else? We have to do something special for your birthday."

"Thanks, Doctor." Zoe grinned, swinging on her mother's hand. "Can we stop and get ice cream on the way?"

Dr. Applewhite chuckled and reached down to swoop Zoe up into her arms. "Of course we can, my darling. Whatever you want. It's your special day. I love you, princess."

"I love you too, Doctor." Zoe giggled happily, surveying the world from her new perch as they moved through the house.

At the window on the landing, Zoe gave a start. There was a mean, ugly face pressed up against the glass. She recognized it: her old mother, the wicked old witch who had tried to lock her up in a castle.

"Why is that person there, Doctor?" she asked, recoiling quickly, burying her head against Dr. Applewhite's hair.

"Where, darling? There's no one at the window, silly," Dr. Applewhite said. "Now, let's get going, or we'll be late."

Zoe looked again as they descended the stairs, trying to get a glimpse to see if she really had been mistaken. Not only was the old witch still there, but she had her mouth open—and from it was coming a horrible blaring noise, repeating over and over, making her want to cover her ears . . .

Zoe awoke with a start, rolling over to hit her cell phone on the bedside table and turn off the alarm. Morning sunlight was streaming through the thin motel curtains, illuminating the room enough for her to read that it was seven in the morning on the wall clock. Time to get up and face the day.

She shivered slightly, rubbing at her face. Her skin still felt tight, her eyelids heavy. All of that crying last night must have done something to it. She still felt a lingering prickling sensation from the dream, the haunting suspense of seeing her mother at the window. Watching them, silently, like a bad omen.

What a strange dream, come to think of it. For the doctor to have been her mother! And yet she didn't even call her Mother, or Mom, or Mommy. Just "Doctor."

Doctor . . .

Zoe swung her legs over the side of the bed, casting around for her watch and phone. She had an idea.

❈ ❈ ❈

Zoe moved confidently across the temporary investigation room they had set up at the sheriff's headquarters, looking for the files they had been going over the day before. "Even if it turns out to be nothing," she was telling Shelley. "I just have a feeling about this."

"Well, any lead is a lead," Shelley sighed. She, too, looked a little worse for wear after their late night. Her normally neat bun was a little misshapen at the back of her head, and darker circles were visible under her eyes even through her makeup. "At this point, we have to take anything we can use."

Zoe found the paperwork she was looking for and leafed through it. "Here we are. All right, I'll give them a call now."

Shelley nodded. "I'll head over to the sheriff's office and see if he has the coroner's report back on the latest victim yet."

Zoe gave her a wave of agreement with the desk telephone against her ear, waiting for it to connect. It rang four times—enough for Zoe to start thinking about hanging up and trying again later—before it was answered.

"Hello?"

"Hello—Marlene Griffiths?"

"No." A snuffle over the receiver. "This is Scarlet, her daughter."

"Scarlet—yes. This is Special Agent Zoe Prime with the FBI. We met yesterday."

"I remember." A brief pause. "Do you have any information about Ivy? Did you catch the guy who ...?"

"No, unfortunately not. I was actually looking for some information from you."

"Oh." Scarlet sounded deflated. "Of course. I'll help if I can."

"You mentioned that your sister was coming back from a doctor's appointment yesterday. Do you happen to know the name and address of the doctor?"

"Oh, yeah. Hang on, let me think ... it was a new guy, she hadn't seen him before. Hold on just a second."

There was a rustling noise from the other end of the line, and Zoe waited patiently in new silence.

"Okay, I've got it," Scarlet said, lifting the receiver again. Zoe could picture her movements from the sound. "She wrote it on the family calendar. Dr. George Smith."

Zoe almost rolled her eyes. Good luck doing a background search on that name. "Do you know the address of his practice?"

"Yeah, it's somewhere out in Eastonville."

Zoe paused, frowning. She was doing the mental calculations. "Eastonville? But that's over an hour's drive away from you. Is Dr. Smith a specialist?"

"I think he's just an OB/GYN," Scarlet said. "Ivy said it was worth the drive, though. She didn't want to go to the local one here."

Zoe thought back. She had lived out here, knew how it could get in these more rural communities. But having to drive so far, when you lived near larger townships that had their own local hospitals? That didn't sound right. There was something about this doctor that got her attention, like a thread sticking out of a sleeve. It was begging to be pulled.

"Did she tell you why she stopped going to the local doctor?" she asked.

"The doctor here was basically a major creep. Ivy said she hated going to him, so she looked for another one elsewhere. She said she was going to check him out and let me know for when I needed to make appointments in the future."

Basically a major creep...? That could have meant a lot of different things, and there was no sense in wasting time on a second-hand source of information. To carry on pulling this thread, Zoe would need to go to the horse's mouth. Since Ivy couldn't give them her account anymore, maybe there was another way. "What's the name of that doctor? The creep?" she asked.

"Oh, I don't know," Scarlet said. "I hadn't had my first test with him yet. Ivy said not to go there, so I didn't bother learning his name."

"Thanks, Scarlet," Zoe said. It wasn't likely to be very difficult to track him down. "You have been very helpful. I will be back in touch as soon as we have any more information to share."

Zoe barely heard the girl's goodbye as she put the phone back in its cradle, thinking. It wasn't necessarily connected, of course, but someone being accused of creepy behavior in a county that suddenly saw a rash of killings was enough of a coincidence to warrant looking into. In her experience, things were rarely just coincidences—more like cause and effect.

"No luck on the coroner's report," Shelley said, coming back into the room and throwing a piece of paper down onto their organized files. "There's no real new information. Everything just like before—he took a few strokes to cut off the head, then left with it. No real signs of a prior struggle except for a few marks on Ivy Griffiths's hands and arms from the corn. That's all."

"There's something," Zoe said, squinting thoughtfully at the screen of the ancient PC the sheriff had loaned them. "Ivy was going to see an OB/GYN. Only, she had to travel far out of town because the local doctor here was, according to her sister, a major creep. Seems like it might be worth looking into, at least a little bit."

"That does sound odd." Shelley frowned. "Do you have his name?"

"No, but he's local to them, so he shouldn't be too hard to find," Zoe said. "I have the name of the man she went to see instead. It was a recent change in her routine, so we should look into him as well."

"All right," Shelley said decisively, sitting down in front of the FBI-issued laptop they had brought with them and cracking her fingers. "I'll take the creep if you look into the new guy."

Zoe nodded her head—it was a fair deal—and fired up the search engine on the clunky machine in front of her. She entered Dr. George Smith and the town he worked in, and soon had his contact details available.

The internet was a wonderful invention. Not only could you find data about just about anything you wanted, including tracking someone down, but people could also leave a permanent mark of their thoughts and feelings. They tended to be more honest, too—there was something about the anonymity of hiding behind a screen that left inhibitions behind in the real world.

There were plenty of reviews for Dr. George Smith on a popular website that catered to local businesses, and Zoe read through them with interest. There were lots of common threads: that Dr. Smith was a kind and patient man, that he had helped to put his patients at ease, that he had listened to their concerns even when other doctors had dismissed them. There were even reviews from women recommending him after successful fertility treatments and pregnancies during which he kept them reassured and relaxed. He sounded like a good man, at least by his reviews.

"Looks like we have a winner," Shelley said, breaking Zoe's concentration. "This guy really is a creep."

"What do you have?" Zoe asked, looking up.

"There's a news article here from the local paper. Apparently a female patient made an official complaint about him and also forwarded the wording of the complaint to the paper. There are hints that other women are thinking of coming forward as well, and a quote from the hospital board that they've had a number of other reports. His license was suspended pending further investigation about a week ago."

"The timing fits," Zoe mused. "Crazed doctor under stress about his job decides to take it out on his former patients, or perhaps complainants, by murdering them. Or maybe just any woman would do."

"Taking the heads as trophies so they can never badmouth him again." Shelley quirked an eyebrow. "The psychology fits, too. This could well be something."

"The new doctor only has good reviews to his name," Zoe said, closing the web page and getting up. "I say we focus on this guy. What's his name?"

"Dr. Harold Edgerton," Shelley read from her screen. "Apparently he's not too many years away from retirement as it is. That could even work—shallow cuts to the neck because he's an older man without as much strength as he used to have."

Zoe let out a low whistle. She was searching amongst the box of evidence that had been brought over from Michelle Young's house for a diary that she had seen, something that no doubt held her appointments. "Get onto Lorna Troye's sister. See if she knows who her OB/GYN was."

"On it." Shelley sprang into action, starting to flip through records for the sister's number, while Zoe put on gloves and started to carefully read through the pages of Michelle Young's diary. She phased out Shelley's voice while she read, trying to concentrate on the page.

The appointments were sparse, all of them filled out in neat block capitals that reflected Michelle Young's compulsively clean personality. Each of them took the same format: a time written on the appropriate day, then a short phrase or a name to indicate what the appointment was for, and on the facing page, an address if it was deemed necessary. There wasn't much to comment on: dentist appointments, scheduled meetings with friends, the odd exercise class.

And, there: finally, after flipping through four months' worth of dull and uninteresting pages, Zoe found it. A listing to meet Dr. Edgerton at 12.30 p.m. on a Wednesday, presumably while on her lunch break from work. Not only that, but it was only two months prior to her death. Michelle Young had been a patient of Edgerton—and a relatively recent one, at that.

"Thank you, that's very helpful . . . Yes, we will, of course. All right. Thanks, Daphne." Shelley finished speaking and hung up the phone, turning to Zoe with a flush of excitement and wide eyes. "Lorna was a patient of his. Daphne remembered her posting on social media about the appointment, saying that her doctor was creepy and warning other local women not to go to him."

"A public complaint. Quite possible that he would have known about it," Zoe pointed out. "That could make her an easy target."

"And if he was as bad as it seems, it's entirely possible that the others made complaints about him, anonymous or otherwise, direct to the medical board," Shelley agreed.

"Right, then," Zoe said, shrugging her jacket on over her shoulders. "Let's find out where he lives and pay Dr. Edgerton a visit, shall we?"

CHAPTER SEVENTEEN

Zoe glanced sideways at Shelley as they lined themselves up on the step, facing the front door of the house. It was large and modern, fresh yellow brick that hadn't yet seen much fading or damage from the sun and rain, but the architecture was designed to look like something else. Stone columns on either side of the entrance, flanked in turn by topiary trees in large ceramic pots, at odds with the sports car parked on the drive.

It didn't take a genius to see that the man who lived here had a lot of money, and also a sense of grandeur. That in itself wasn't totally unusual for a doctor, but it helped things to stack up. The sense of ego, damaged by complaints and stoked to a frenzy by the question mark over his reputation.

"Hello?" The man who answered the door was in his sixties, with a tall and unbowed back topped by a head of silvered hair. He wore a thick pair of glasses on his face, the lenses like bubbles bulging out of old-fashioned wire frames.

"Dr. Harold Edgerton?" Shelley asked in a pleasant tone.

"Who are you?" he demanded. It wasn't exactly an admission of identity, but in Zoe's experience, those who weren't being asked for by name usually just answered in the negative.

"Special Agent Shelley Rose with the FBI," Shelley said, holding out her badge as Zoe did the same. "This is Special Agent Zoe Prime. May we come inside?"

Edgerton's back straightened like a rod, and he eyed them with an aggressive suspicion. "What for?" he asked brusquely.

"We'd like to have a word with you," Shelley replied, her tone remaining even. "It relates to a number of your patients."

Edgerton looked between the two of them quickly, his eyes narrowing further as his head shook. "What's the FBI want with me? The issue is being dealt with by the medical board."

"We are aware of the complaints against you, Dr. Edgerton," Zoe told him mildly. "However, this is relating to a different matter. Are you aware that several of your patients have recently been murdered?"

The doctor blinked, which was about as good a reaction as they were going to get; it could have been indicative of surprise, but whether it was because he had no idea about the murders or because he hadn't expected them to be linked back to him, Zoe couldn't say. Almost immediately afterwards, a thunderous frown drew two silvery eyebrows down over his eyes, making them pop like bushy caterpillars into the zone of magnification provided by his thick glasses. "You want to question me about murders?"

"As we say," Shelley told him calmly, "perhaps it's best that we do this inside." She gave a pointed look toward one of the neighboring houses.

"I think not," Dr. Edgerton said, drawing himself up yet further and bristling at them like a cat facing down a dog. "I have no interest whatsoever in talking to you. I am facing enough stress as it is."

"It would be a shame to increase that stress by causing a scene," Zoe said. She was beginning to run out of patience very rapidly. "This is a murder investigation, Doctor. You can imagine that we aren't taking it lightly."

"This is just scapegoating," Dr. Edgerton declared. He gestured wildly, pointing as if toward people who were not there. "That sheriff has put you up to this, hasn't he? I'm being targeted. Harassed! Someone in that sheriff's department must have it out for me. Well, I'm not going to stand for it. I'm already facing complaints from all of those stupid women—no doubt coerced. I'm looking at losing my license. I might even be charged! And now you people want to take me in for murders, too? No—I'm not having it." He finished his tirade by crossing his arms solidly across his chest, as if to say that that was his decision and there was no way they were going to change his mind.

"Let's be clear on this, Dr. Edgerton," Shelley said, her tone remaining remarkably smooth in the face of his bluster. "Are you refusing to submit to questioning voluntarily?"

"You're damn right I am," Dr. Edgerton snapped. "So you can go and bother someone else, and get off my doorstep."

Zoe and Shelley exchanged a glance. Whatever was going to happen here, it certainly wasn't going to go down the way that Dr. Edgerton wanted it to. Seeing confirmation in Zoe's eyes, Shelley snapped her head up with new resolve.

"Then, Dr. Edgerton, we're placing you under arrest for suspected murder," she said, even as Zoe stepped forward to take hold of the man's hands and put them behind his back. "You have the right to remain silent and refuse to answer questions. Anything you say may be used against you in a court of law. You have the right to consult an attorney before speaking to the police and to have an attorney present during questioning. If you cannot afford an attorney, one will be appointed for you if you wish. If you decide to talk to us now without an attorney present, you can stop at any time."

"I'm not damn likely to talk to you, attorney or not," the doctor said through gritted teeth.

"Come on," Zoe said, placing a well-practiced hand on his back to encourage him along. "Let's get you in the car."

"Let's start with Michelle Young," Zoe said, placing the file photograph on the table in front of Dr. Edgerton. Beside him, a stiff-suited attorney with gray hair waited silently, a gold pen and pad of paper in front of him. "Do you recognize this woman?"

"Of course I do," Dr. Edgerton said dismissively. "She was one of my patients."

"Why do you say 'was,' Doctor?" Zoe asked. It was a well-documented slip-up: the killer, who knew the victim was dead, would refer to them in the past tense automatically, while someone who did not know would still use present tense.

"Because I don't have any patients anymore," Dr. Edgerton sneered. "Or were you hoping I was about to give you a confession? You said this was about murders, and I've seen her face on the news, anyway."

"All right." Zoe bit her tongue. All she wanted to do was walk out of this room and leave Dr. Edgerton to his own devices. The man was infuriating. Still, this had to be done a certain way: find out if the killer knew the victims, check for alibis, start pushing for a confession if guilt was still likely. It was the only way forward, and only she and Shelley could do it. This was an FBI investigation, after all. "How about these two?"

She laid out the pictures of Lorna Troye and Ivy Griffiths, smiling and happy in life. Carefree. It was always the nicest images that families gave to police, to give a face to their loved ones that would make an impact with the press.

Dr. Edgerton made a scoffing noise. "I know them."

Shelley leaned forward slightly across the table. Zoe, recognizing that her partner had caught a scent to follow, stayed silent. "How do you know them, Dr. Edgerton?"

"They are also my patients." He glanced over the images again. "This one was on the news as well. But not her. Ivy Griffiths. She's dead as well, is she?"

"You don't seem very upset to learn that," Shelley pointed out.

"Well, I'm not. Damn evil bitches. They're the ones that put in complaints against me."

There was a pause, a note of silence hanging in the room. The lawyer shifted in his chair, raising his hand to tap his client on the shoulder. He whispered something to him: Zoe couldn't fully catch it, but it sounded a lot like *language choices* and *self-incriminating*.

"How do you know they're the ones who made complaints?" Shelley asked. "Those reports are supposed to be kept confidential from the accused."

"Well, it's not hard to work out, is it?" Dr. Edgerton scoffed again, giving them both a superior look. "They splash these things all over public internet pages. Anyway, I've got a friend on the board."

Zoe frowned at him. "I would like to know the name of this friend," she said. "Sharing information like that would be a serious breach of privacy laws."

Edgerton tossed his head pompously, ignoring a nudging from his lawyer. "I'm friends with most of the board," he said. "Good luck trying to pin down which one of them it was."

Zoe put that aside for now. It was irritating, certainly, but that was all. The local PD would maybe find out who it was at some point, maybe give them a slap on the wrist. She had bigger fish to fry. And, thankfully, bigger bait to use: while Edgerton had been going through the booking process and waiting for his lawyer to arrive, Zoe and Shelley had put the time to good use.

"You know, it doesn't actually surprise us to hear that you knew who your accusers were," Zoe said, giving a minute hand gesture toward Shelley to indicate that it was time to show him the next thing. "You see, we have already done a bit of asking around. It seems that you got into a bit of a public altercation with Ms. Griffiths."

Edgerton shifted in his seat, glancing edgewise at his lawyer. "What of it?"

Shelley placed an image in front of him that had been taken from a grainy cell phone video, shot by someone there on the scene. "We saw a very interesting video recording of the altercation in question," Zoe told him. She kept her voice calm and measured, almost dead of inflection. Shelley had her ways of getting people to talk, mostly based on making them feel comfortable and soothed. Zoe had her own. She had noted on more than one occasion that others became unnerved when she acted like an emotionless robot, unflustered by anything. At Shelley's encouragement, she had decided that now was as good a time as any to try to use that. "You weren't very happy with her, were you?"

She took out her own cell phone and placed it flat on the table between them, tapping the screen. A recording began to play: Dr. Edgerton and Ivy Griffiths, standing opposite one another in what looked like a parking lot, confrontationally close. Whoever recorded it had only been able to start filming after the altercation had already begun, but it was enough.

"How dare you?" Ivy's voice demanded, echoing out from the speakers to ghostly effect. *"You aren't supposed to know who put in a formal complaint."*

"I know it was you," Dr. Edgerton said, his face contorted with fury. *"You stupid bitch. Your little lies have them threatening to take my license away. Recant your statement!"*

"I haven't lied about anything!" Ivy was refusing to back down, standing her ground. *"Watch yourself, old man. This is harassment. Kind of proves my point, doesn't it?"*

"If you don't take it back, you stupid bitch, I'll see you in the fucking ground," Edgerton growled. His face was inches away from Ivy's, his fists clenched.

"All right, all right, there's witnesses here!" the person behind the camera called out. *"You touch her, we're going straight to the police."*

"We're going to the police anyway," Ivy said, eyeing Edgerton with a bold and cruel smile. *"I'm not scared of you. You're just a creepy old man. And I'm not going to let you put your hands on any more women."*

In the video, Edgerton growled and stalked away, pushing the camera away from him with a vicious motion before disappearing into the distance. The video recorded for a few more moments, turning back to a flushed and clearly shaken Ivy, before ending.

"You threatened Ms. Griffiths's life," Zoe said, pointing to the still final frame of the video. "This was, what? Only a week before she was murdered in cold blood?"

Dr. Edgerton's face had gone a shade paler and there was something more slack about the angle of his jaw. Beside him, the lawyer cleared his throat, perhaps to remind his client of something they had discussed in private.

"That was said in the heat of the moment," Edgerton said. "But I never laid a hand on her. You can see it in the video for yourself. I just walked away. I'm not a man of physical violence."

"She made you angry, though, didn't she?" Shelley said, leaning forward over the table. "She made you feel powerless. Nothing you could do to stop her from ruining your career. Her and the others."

"Well, it's not fair," Edgerton said, sounding like nothing more than an overgrown baby. "I studied for years for my medical degree, spent years practicing. I've saved lives. One complaint, and I'm on the scrap heap. Think of all the people that might not get the help they need, without me there!"

"You were very angry, weren't you?" Shelley pressed.

"Angry, yes. Of course. But not *homicidal*."

"They called you a creep," Shelley taunted him. "They dragged your reputation through the mud. Said you touched them in ways you didn't need to. That you dragged out the examinations. Made them feel like a piece of meat on a slab. They told their friends, their family members. Everyone knows."

Edgerton's face was turning red. "I didn't do any of that," he blustered. "I'm an upstanding member of this community. I have a teenage daughter. It's all nonsense."

"I think it's the truth," Shelley said slyly. "I think you're a creep who should have his medical license stripped. I wouldn't trust you if you were my doctor."

Edgerton slammed his hand against the edge of the table, spit flying from his mouth as he shouted, "I am an innocent man. This is trial by gossip!"

The lawyer laid a hand on his client's arm, but Shelley was already sitting smugly back in her chair. She'd gotten the emotional reaction she wanted. Zoe took that as a cue to move on.

"I'd like an account of your whereabouts yesterday," Zoe said. "Where were you in the early hours of the afternoon?"

Dr. Edgerton bristled, but he managed to maintain his cool enough to answer. "I was sitting at home, thinking about all the ways my life has just been ruined. Does that satisfy you?"

"Can anyone verify that? Your daughter, perhaps?"

"She lives with her mother in Rhode Island," Dr. Edgerton snapped. "I was alone. I should have been at work, if it wasn't for this ridiculous campaign."

"Interesting." Zoe flipped back a page in her notebook, consulted the estimated times and dates of death for the other two women. "Have you had many appointments this week, Dr. Edgerton?"

"No. I've been sitting at home with the curtains closed so I can't see all my neighbors gossiping about me." Edgerton sulked, looking at the edge of the table. Even he seemed to be slowly grasping the fact that things didn't look good for him. "I've been alone the whole time. I went out shopping last Monday and everyone stared at me, so I've been living off things from the back of the cupboard, putting off going out again. Does that satisfy you?"

"Very much so," Zoe said, rising to get out of her seat. "My colleague and I have a lot to discuss, thanks to you. We'll see you soon, Dr. Edgerton. I suggest you use this time to consult with your lawyer."

She swept out of the room with Shelley following her, inwardly grinning with success—though outwardly as stony-faced as ever.

"Do you think we've got him?" Shelley asked, spinning around as soon as the door had closed behind them.

"What does your gut say?" Zoe asked.

"He's got motive and no alibi. He sounds good to me," Shelley said. "With the threat to Ivy's life thrown in, we've got more than enough grounds to hold him on suspicion of murder, even without a confession."

"He's the right height and weight, too," Zoe mused. "His age would explain the multiple lighter strokes to the neck. I don't see anything in the numbers that makes me think he doesn't fit the bill."

"Then, you think we've got the right man?" Shelley asked. There was a hopefulness in her voice which suggested she had already convinced herself as much.

Zoe closed her eyes, seeing Ivy Griffiths's body in her head. The video. The mere inch of space between their noses as they confronted one another, the footprints in the mud... Edgerton was even the right shoe size, and local knowledge would have been extremely helpful for getting in and out of the farm's lands without being seen.

"I think we have him," Zoe confirmed. "Now we just have to make him crack."

CHAPTER EIGHTEEN

Zoe stepped up onto the hastily erected podium outside the sheriff's station, trying not to look down at the sea of reporters in front of her. It was only a small town, but apparently news outlets from across the state and the nation had come to hear what she had to say. That didn't help the feeling of pressure.

"We have arrested a suspect in connection with the murders of three local women," she said, focusing on the statement that was typed out in front of her. If she did that and pretended she was terrible at memorization—which, of course, she wasn't—then she didn't have to look up as often. She didn't have to see the news cameras trained on her, the flashes of photographers, the expectant faces and upheld voice recorders of journalists. "That suspect will remain in custody for further questioning and we will release more details as and when we can. For now, though, we believe we may have the killer off the streets."

Zoe looked up for a moment, then wished she hadn't. There were so many faces staring back at her. Just behind her on either side were Shelley and Sheriff Hawthorne, backing her up. Still, it was hardly enough to make her feel reassured. Having this much attention on her made her feel like an alien, even now. That she was going to slip up, drop the human façade in some small and unknowable way, and everyone would see that she was different.

She dropped her gaze back down to the paper. Now was not the time to start getting distracted with calculating the zoom length of the lenses or working out the angle of the sun and the ISO level they could drop down to thanks to the brightness of its rays.

"Although we have made significant process in this case, we are asking that the women of Nebraska do not let down their guard just yet. Our advice is to stay vigilant. Avoid being out and about on your own. Go with company if you can. Do not engage with strangers, especially males. Now is not a time to relax—not until we have the killer ready to be prosecuted in a court of law. As we continue the questioning phase, we want to be wary of giving too positive a message, particularly when the possibility that the killer is still out there is very real."

Zoe took a breath, looking up at the reporters. Now, for the part she liked the least: having to think and talk on her feet, right in front of live video feeds. "I will now take questions from the press."

A young woman with a prim, fitted, size two skirt suit shot her hand in the air. "Amy Belfast, *Nebraska Times*. Can you tell us the identity of the suspect in custody?"

"At this time, all I can tell you is that we have arrested a sixty-one-year-old male."

"Aiden West, *Broken Ridge Gazette*. How confident are you that you have arrested the right man? You're giving us mixed messages." This, from a man in the front row with horn-rimmed glasses.

"We have every reason to believe we have the right suspect in custody," Zoe said. "At this moment, we are simply staying cautious. For example, it's not out of the question for there to have been an accomplice working alongside our suspect who is still out there." That was a little bit of a white lie: in truth, she had seen no evidence of a collaborator, but she had also learned a long time ago to be wary of delivering absolutes—especially to the press.

There were more questions after that, enough of them that they started to blend together. Zoe repeated herself at least three times: it was an old press conference trick. Keep to a simple statement and repeat when you don't want to give away any more details. It was not dissimilar to a tactic that was taught to members of the armed forces who were in danger of being kidnapped and tortured for information. Which, Zoe mused, was a little close to how it felt to be interrogated by the press.

"That will be all for now," she said eventually, holding up a hand. "I and my colleague, Special Agent Shelley Rose, will be remaining here in Broken Ridge to progress the investigation of the case. We'll call another press conference should any more important information arise."

She turned to Shelley, who nodded, and they stepped down from the podium together. "Well done," Shelley whispered. "They were like dogs with bones. How long do you think it will take before they manage to connect the dots and name the doctor?"

"Oh, they'll already know his name," Zoe said grimly. She'd had enough dealings with the press to know that some reporter would have been on the doorsteps of Dr. Edgerton's neighbors within half an hour of him being taken away. "They were just trying to confirm it."

"Well, for once, I can't say I'll be sorry if we accidentally get an innocent man's name dragged through the mud," Shelley declared. "Even if he's not the killer—which I'm fairly sure he is—Dr. Edgerton deserves it."

Though she agreed, Zoe kept quiet. The case wasn't done yet. There was still the matter of a confession—and if they didn't get that, plus a guilty plea when it came to trial, they would be staying in Nebraska for a longer time than she would have liked. Which was no time at all, because she had already been too close to her childhood home for far too long.

"Let's get back to our suspect," she said. "See if he feels like telling us the truth now."

He reached for his sandwich and took a bite, enjoying the flavors. Crisp lettuce, tangy sauce, smokey ham, juicy tomato. It was good. She had picked a nice place. She always did. Her taste was impeccable, always.

His girlfriend sat opposite him, a glint in her eyes as she watched him take a bite. "Good?" she asked, picking slowly at her own plate, bringing a stray leaf to her mouth between manicured fingers.

He nodded, swallowing quickly to answer. "It's really good. How do you find these places?"

She gave him a coy smile, another spark in her eyes. "I have my ways," she said. She was never one for giving too much away. She liked keeping a bit of mystery, she had told him.

He shook his head with a grin, then took another bite. He knew from experience that there was no use in trying to press her into revealing more. If she didn't want to tell him something, then all he would manage was to rile her up. He didn't like it when they argued. She was wild and hot when she yelled, like a whirlwind that he could not resist, but it was still a jolt of pain to have her mad at him. He never wanted to disappoint her or let her down. They were meant to be together, and he wouldn't allow anything to jeopardize that—even his own self.

"How long until you have to go meet your friend?" he asked.

She checked her watch. "Twenty minutes."

His heart sank. It was always a wrench to have to leave her. Of course, he had his own things to attend to, both the secret and mysterious and the ordinary. There were things he did that he wouldn't have wanted her to witness. But if all things were equal and he could somehow reconcile the two parts of his life, he would have preferred to have her with him at all times.

"Better make the most of it then," he said, forcing a smile over the top of his glass of fruit juice that she had insisted was good for his heart and his health.

Over her head, there was a television mounted on the wall, providing some entertainment for the assembled patrons. Some were sitting underneath it to watch it more closely, while others ignored it entirely. His eyes flicked idly over it and then stopped, frozen. What was this, now...?

Two women were on the screen, one at the forefront and the other slightly behind, both wearing FBI-branded jackets. On the other side there was the sheriff, easily recognizable in his hat and his dust-colored shirt. They were holding a press conference, it seemed. The set-up was standard: a small podium for the agent to lean on as she spoke, the others gathered behind her, press assembled in front. Flashes from cameras occasionally went off and painted her boyish features with harsh light.

The sound was off, but subtitles ran across the bottom of the screen, spelling out everything the agent was saying. He watched closely, reading as he took another bite of his sandwich, no longer really tasting it.

She was saying that they had a suspect in custody for the three murdered women.

He almost bit his tongue. Those were his kills. His victims. Being ascribed to someone else.

How did that feel? He tilted his head to the side a moment, considering. It was good luck; he would have to be a fool not to see that. It took the heat away from him. But on the other hand, it meant that all of the credit for his hard work was going to someone else. Which didn't sit well with him at all.

To be given credit, or to escape justice...? Well, of course, the second option was far and away the best. It meant he would be able to stay with his girlfriend, perhaps make her his wife. That was the most pleasing option by a thousand miles. But that didn't mean that someone else had to claim the credit.

He could escape justice just as easily without having another man behind bars for what he had done.

It wasn't that he felt bad for this man, whoever he was. It made no difference to him if a stranger was free or imprisoned. It was the credit that rankled.

"What are you looking at?" his girlfriend asked.

His eyes flickered down to meet hers for a moment. "Just an interesting news story," he said.

She turned in her chair and began to watch along with him. "Oh, they've caught someone," she said, catching up by reading the breaking news script at the bottom of the screen. "That's good news."

"Mm," he agreed, unsure if he really did.

The press conference ended, the FBI agents turning away from the cameras before the view changed abruptly. A reporter was standing some distance away from the area where the press conference had been held, now wrapping up behind her. She held a microphone below her mouth, fixing the camera with a direct stare.

"That was FBI agents Zoe Prime and Shelley Rose, along with Sheriff Hawthorne, giving us an update on the string of grisly beheadings that have plagued rural Nebraska this week," she said.

He stopped reading, tuning out the rest. Zoe Prime and Shelley Rose. Very interesting. It wouldn't hurt to know more about those two, would it?

He didn't need to write anything down. He'd made a mental note of their names. His girlfriend turned back around and returned her attention to her plate, and he did the same.. He was no longer upset at the prospect of their lunch date coming to an end. He had work to do, and it would be better to start as soon as possible.

Chapter Nineteen

Zoe paused on the way into the sheriff's station, fumbling in her pocket for her buzzing cell phone. She held it up in front of her for long enough to see that it was a number from their headquarters, the J. Edgar Hoover Building back in D.C., before putting it up to her ear.

"Special Agent Zoe Prime," she said, holding up a hand to Shelley to tell her to wait.

"Zoe." The voice on the other end of the line was their superior, SAIC Leo Maitland. It was not unexpected that he would call. Shelley had turned in some paperwork before the press conference and notified him that they were holding it. "Good work. I was watching live."

"Thank you, sir," Zoe said, stepping to one side in order to clear the path for the sheriff's men returning to their workplace. "We're confident that we have our man."

"As am I," Maitland told her. "It looks like the case is all wrapped up. I'm calling you back to D.C. this afternoon. The locals can take over from here and get their confession. I don't want to waste a couple of my best agents on questioning—there's enough evidence against him from what I read, and they can get it in front of a judge without your help."

Zoe tried to pretend that she didn't feel a girlish thrill of satisfaction at the phrase "best agents." "We will prepare for the flights," she said, a mechanical response really; she had never been good at either small talk or responding to praise. Still, she hoped that he could tell from the inflection she tried to put into her voice that she was pleased.

Beside her, Shelley grinned. She was, no doubt, ecstatic to hear that she would be returning to her family soon.

"You'll have the flight details via email," Maitland continued. "Check back in with the office if any trouble arises. We'll see you back in first thing tomorrow morning for a full debrief."

"First thing, sir," Zoe confirmed.

"Good work," Maitland said again, before she heard the click and sudden silence of an ended call.

"We're going home soon?" Shelley asked immediately, clearly hungry for details.

"Flight details over email," Zoe relayed. "And he said we did a good job. Twice."

Shelley grinned even wider. She was already searching through her emails, tapping impatiently on the screen to get it to load faster. "Here we are. We've got just over three hours to get everything ready."

"All right," Zoe said. The heavy feeling that seemed to be part and parcel of an ongoing case was already dissipating, replaced by the rush and surge of urgency, of the need to organize things quickly and get gone. She was going to leave Nebraska, get away from all of these memories and ghosts. The thought filled her with a heady elation. She was going home.

"I'll tell the sheriff," Shelley said, springing forward with a gleeful enthusiasm. Zoe let her go. She hesitated outside in the sun, turning around in a circle, squinting her eyes against the bright sky. This place was not her home. It hadn't been when she was younger, and it meant even less to her now.

But something had changed during her visit here—something irrevocable. Even though her mother had died years before without her knowledge, knowing it was something else. Being back here had changed something, too. She had been afraid for a long time, she realized, of this place and what it meant to her. That dragon had perhaps been subdued, if not entirely slayed. It was hard to be afraid of a place that no longer held anything waiting for you.

She knew in her heart that she would never come here again, except in the line of work. There was nothing left to see, nothing left to say. She had no curiosity or desire to see any other relatives. A chapter of her life had closed for good, beyond anyone's reach.

There was something else, too—a change in her worldview, a realization that things were better said sooner. She worked with death every day, but it was funny how the death of someone you actually knew could change your outlook. The people who actually mattered needed to know that they did.

Shelley bounded back out of the station, her blonde hair dazzling in the sun. She flashed Zoe an equally dazzling smile on her way past, zooming toward their rental car. "Come on, Z!" she said. "Time to get packed up. I'll tell you this, I'm not going to miss that shabby motel at all."

Zoe had to laugh. She followed quickly, getting behind the wheel and starting up the engine. There was no sense of nostalgia as she pulled away, leaving the sheriff and his men behind for the last time. Only a gladness. Just like Shelley, she had someone to go home to now. Someone she was looking forward to seeing.

"Come knock on my door when you're ready to go," Shelley said as they pulled up. "We need to set off for the airport in two hours to make it in time, but I don't mind hanging out there instead of here. I might get some new perfume or something to treat myself. And candy for Amelia. She loves it when I bring home the little regional containers, you know?"

"I think she might just like the candy," Zoe said, chuckling.

"Fine. I like collecting the regional containers," Shelley shot over her shoulder on the way to her motel room. "I've got a nice stack of tins going. See you in a bit."

Zoe nodded, heading for her own room and unlocking the door for the last time. It felt good. Going home, getting certain things sorted out. Things were going to be better from now on.

It did not take her long at all to gather up her things from around the small room: spare suits hanging in the wardrobe, underwear in a drawer, one pair of boots wrapped up in a plastic bag to avoid getting dirt on anything else, toiletries from the bathroom, dirty clothes in a laundry bag, a few other small essentials. She was practiced at the art of packing and unpacking, and everything fit perfectly in their assigned places in her small travel suitcase. She gave the room a once-over, checking she had not left anything behind, and hesitated in the bathroom, seeing herself in the mirror.

She had never considered herself to be pretty. She had a boyish face, not helped by the short-cropped brown hair around it. For a brief moment she wondered what she would look like if she allowed it to grow longer, like Shelley, but she dismissed the thought. That wasn't her. She was who she was, and she was no longer ashamed of that.

She wore two small studs in her ears, designed to try to soften and feminize her face a little—something that she had noticed male law enforcement officials responded more warmly to. She reached up and took them out, tucking them away into a small case so that they would not bother her on the plane. She tried out a smile in the mirror, an old habit of practice. It wasn't so bad. She even looked almost human if she concentrated hard enough.

All of this, she knew, was an avoidance exercise. She was already having fluttering palpitations in her chest now that she thought about the reality of her decision. She had resolved to tell John her secret—to let him know about the numbers that she saw everywhere. He had perhaps already guessed that she was not quite like other people, but it was also important that he understand exactly how. It was time. If they were to take their relationship any further, he deserved to know.

One thing she couldn't do was have the conversation over the phone. But judging by how nervous it made her feel to even think of the idea of telling him, she wasn't sure her nerve would hold once she saw him again in person. She had to do something—something that would stop herself from backing out once she was home.

She pulled out her cell phone and stared at his number, thinking. Seeing her family members again had done nothing so efficiently as to remind her that it was the family she chose, not the one she was born with, that really mattered. Dr. Applewhite, Shelley, John. The ones she trusted and wanted to have around her. She needed to keep them around her, make sure that they knew how much she appreciated them.

And that started with them knowing the truth about her. Shelley and Dr. Applewhite had both been in the loop for a long time, but John was still effectively on the outside of her circle of trust. He needed to know, but she needed just as much to see his face, to read his reaction. As little as she could manage to read the emotions of others, she was at least better off when she had facial expressions and body language to go by instead of just a voice. She needed to know what he would really think of her. Whether he would be disgusted or excited, proud or no longer interested.

She hit the call button before she could change her mind, lifting the cell to her ear and waiting. In order to prevent herself from putting the phone down before he answered, she busied herself with opening the motel room door and stepping outside. The clear sunshine hit her in the face, the warmth, and this time she felt a little better for it.

"Hello, you," John said, answering the call with a tone of surprise and delight. "I wasn't expecting to hear from you yet. Are you back?"

"No, we're about to get on the flight," Zoe said, shading her eyes to look out beyond the parking lot and across to a green vista of fields and farms before, in the distance, the next town. "I thought I would give you a call as we have a couple of hours to wait."

"Are you calling to tell me you're on the way home?" John asked. His voice was expressive enough that she could tell he was smiling. "I could get used to this."

Zoe stifled a laugh. "No, actually, I was calling to tell you I want to talk to you as soon as I am home," she said. "It cannot wait until the weekend. Tomorrow evening, as soon as I get off work."

"All right." John sounded more serious now. "What is it about?"

"I will tell you then," Zoe said. "Otherwise there would be no point in arranging the time to talk."

"I take your point," John said. "Ah, Zoe ... it's not ... I mean ..."

"Will you be available?" Zoe asked. She hadn't meant to cut him off, but then again he didn't seem to be going anywhere. Whatever it was that he didn't want to spit out, she couldn't wait forever.

"Yes, I will," John said. "I guess I'll see you then. Where should we meet?"

Zoe hesitated; she didn't have an immediate answer in mind. The meeting itself had been the most urgent point, not the place. "How about the bar we went to the first time we met?" she suggested. It had been the first thing she thought of, but now that she considered it a bit more, perhaps there was a nice sense of a closing circle about it. The place where their relationship had first begun to blossom would now be the place where it rose to the next level—or ended, depending on John's reaction.

"Sounds great. And what time, exactly?"

There was something about John's tone that sounded slightly off now, though Zoe wasn't sure if she was imagining it. He didn't know yet what she was going to say, of course. He might be nervous about it. She would have to let him suffer, for just a day and a bit. She couldn't give him a preview of what she wanted to discuss. It wasn't that simple.

She could only hope that he would understand.

CHAPTER TWENTY

Shelley hummed happily to herself as she carefully folded up her clothes, placing them neatly in her suitcase. She took care to place a framed photograph of her husband and daughter, which she always traveled with, between two layers of clothing to keep it safe from smashing.

She thought excitedly of getting home in time to see Harry, even if Amelia would already be in bed. She had missed him as she always did, even though it had only been a few days. Family was the most important thing in the world to her, and though she loved her job, she loved coming home to them even more.

She took out her cell phone and sent a quick text to Harry, letting him know to expect her home that night. She included the details of her flight; Harry liked to track her journey home, and if she was flying in the daytime, he would always let Amelia watch the illustration of a plane moving across the map to chart her progress.

This had been a good case, she reflected, folding her FBI-branded jacket up on top of everything else. They had come in and solved it quickly, with only one more victim lost before they were able to bring the killer in. That was a good record. Having no further deaths would have been better, of course, but cases that required the assistance of the FBI were rarely straightforward.

Zoe, too, had come on leaps and bounds. Shelley smiled to herself, thinking of how she had handled the interrogation. She was learning faster than Shelley would have thought. All of this time struggling, and all she really needed was a sympathetic ear to tell her she was doing fine and help her to see how to use the skills she already had. A lifetime of observing others and imitating their behavior to try to fit in had shown her everything she needed to know. All Shelley had done was to help her see beyond the numbers, and even that she couldn't take full credit for.

Before long, Zoe was going to be such a crack investigator that she wouldn't even need a partner. Not that Shelley was afraid she would be cast off. Zoe wasn't like that. She was a good person.

Shelley was almost done with packing up everything; she checked all of the drawers, even though she hadn't put anything in them in the first place, as well as the wardrobe, under the pillows, and under the bed itself. There was no telling what she might leave behind if she didn't check—a maid could easily have knocked something to the floor or hidden it away in the name of neatness.

Satisfied that the whole of the bedroom was dealt with, except for the suitcase itself still propped open on the bed, she opened the bathroom door and went inside to gather her toiletries from there.

Shelley was so caught up in her task that she didn't have the time to react when something—someone—leapt out from behind the shower curtain, sweeping it aside in a rattle of metal hoops against a metal bar and jumping toward her. There was a blur of something swinging toward her and then an impact that rattled her skull and sank her to the floor, the cold tile of the bathroom only vaguely registering. Her head throbbed—something caught an echo in her memory—the case—the girls had been subdued by something before being beheaded, knocked to the ground—

Shelley opened her eyes again, realizing that they were closed, and tried to look around. She was lying face down on the floor, but no one was in front of her. She blinked, trying to clear her vision. She could see two of everything, two grids of lines stretching in front of her face where two sets of tile patterns overlaid one another, confusing her sense of depth perception.

Where was he? She managed to sit up and turn, moving back out into the motel room proper. She had already packed her gun away, zipped up safely inside the inner compartment of her suitcase. She wasn't supposed to need it. There were shadows and lights running across her face and she couldn't make sense of any of them, except that she knew she was in immediate danger and that she had to get to that gun at all costs.

No. There he was, a dark figure of a man that she couldn't get her eyes to focus on, standing by the bed. Watching her crawling. He was between her and the suitcase. The gun was gone. Out of her reach. She had to think of something else.

"Where do you think you're going?" he asked. His voice was so normal. So human. She thought of Harry.

Without the gun she was helpless. Shelley knew she would need someone else—someone whose head wasn't throbbing, who wasn't seeing two of everything, who couldn't feel the slow trickle of something warm and wet down the back of their neck. She needed Zoe. Zoe, who was in the room next door, packing her bags.

She would come and knock on the door when she was done.

Shelley managed to raise herself half onto her knees, fighting to be upright, to at least keep moving. If she could move toward the door, maybe, if she could reach the window—

She saw Zoe outside, standing in the parking lot with her hand to her ear. Talking. She had her back to the motel, but Shelley would recognize that cropped brown hair anywhere, that particular stance that Zoe had, that crumpled suit jacket. *Zoe*, she thought desperately, but no sound came out of her open mouth.

Turn around, she begged silently. Whatever had happened to her head had broken something in her, and she couldn't speak at all, only issue a strange low groan that at first she did not even identify as coming from herself. *Turn around and see me.* But Zoe was facing away.

"I asked you a question," he said. He sounded bored. This was all a game to him. Shelley knew that from the crime scenes. He would take his time. He never felt rushed or panicked. She had a window, a small window now, to do something, to act—

If she could break the window, the sound of the breaking glass would make Zoe look around. Even if she could hit it hard enough to make a loud thud, maybe.

What could she use? Everything was put away in her suitcase! But there—there on the desk that sat under the window—there was the phone. The motel's landline, installed to allow customers to make calls. If she could reach that—grab it up—throw it against the glass—even if he managed to catch hold of her then—

She reached up, but even as she did so, a heavy weight hit her back and she sprawled across the floor again. Shelley knew she was done. If Zoe didn't by coincidence turn and see a strange man in Shelley's room, she was done.

The point of a toe dug into her ribs and she felt herself flipping over, landing on her back. When her skull hit the floor there was a flash of pain, blindingly white, that removed everything else from her for a moment. When it faded away she realized she was making that sound again, that long, guttural groan, and with some effort managed to stop.

"Your manners don't match your neat looks, do they, Agent Michelle Rose?" he asked. She saw him swim into her vision again, wobbly and blurred, too difficult to focus on. There was a weight in the center of her body. That same foot, maybe. The strangest little things caught on her mind. She tried to work out what it was that held her down, her hands fluttering toward it to pull it away.

"Never mind," he grunted. "I guess you're not much into conversation today. I suppose we'll call that an end to our little chat."

Through the blur and the queasiness that was overcoming her she saw the flash of something in his hand and she knew. She knew it was the machete, she knew it was coming for her neck. She closed her eyes at the last moment, not wanting to see the thing that would be her death.

Chapter Twenty One

"Have a safe flight, Zoe," John said, before ending the call.

Zoe paused for a moment, tapping her cell against her lips, thinking. It was done now. There was no way she could wiggle out of this one. One way or another, she was going to tell him the truth—and find out just how much of a Mr. Right John was.

She turned back to the motel. She was fully packed and ready, nothing left to do. She walked over to Shelley's door as they had agreed, and knocked on it, waiting to hear a response.

Nothing. That was odd. Shelley had been excited to go. Zoe thought she would have been champing at the bit by now—she was surprised, in fact, that her partner hadn't come over and tapped her on the shoulder while she was on the phone, wanting to get in the car. She knocked again and waited, but heard nothing at all.

She leaned a little closer, straining her ears. There was no sound coming from inside the room whatsoever. That was very strange. Maybe Shelley had seen she was on the phone and gone across to the motel office while Zoe wasn't looking? She hefted her cell in her hands again and dialed Shelley's number.

There was a pause while the line connected, and then a ringing noise—coming from the motel room. Zoe recognized it as the ringtone that Shelley had activated on her cell. She was still in the room, then. So why wasn't she answering? Zoe waited impatiently, but the phone rang through to voicemail. She ended the call, frowning to herself.

Maybe Shelley was in the shower? She hadn't said anything about stopping to wash up—they were about to get on a flight, after all, so it didn't really make sense. Still, strange things could happen. Maybe Shelley had knocked a bottle of something over herself while she was packing up and wanted to wash it off.

Zoe lingered, wondering what to do. Should she wait? How long for? Shelley had been clear about wanting to get to the airport as quickly as possible. The last thing Zoe wanted was some kind of comedy of errors where they both sat waiting for one another inside their separate motel rooms until the two hours was up and they had to go.

She stepped to the side, glancing in through the window. The blinds were only slightly parted, and the room inside was dark, in contrast to the brightness of the outside. It took a moment for her eyes to adjust. Before she could make out anything in the interior, her eyes glanced down to a speck of something on the edge of the blind. Something...

Zoe snapped to attention, moving back to the door and hammering loudly on it. "Shelley?" she yelled, pausing only to wait to hear an answer. There was none. She lost her patience and kicked at the door; it was cheap and thin-looking, but it bounced back against her kick, sending a ricochet of pain up the length of her leg and into her hip. It didn't matter. She needed to get inside. She needed to get the door open, because what she had seen was—

She kicked again and again, cursing between shouts of Shelley's name, feeling the pain shoot through her again and again, until finally a shower of splinters burst away from the lock and the door swung open. It clattered against the back wall and began to swing back before Zoe rushed forward, springing into the room and then—

And then stopping, staring, because it was all she could do.

The blood was everywhere. Great splashes and sprays of it, coating the bed, the suitcase, the carpet, the walls. It was splashed up the side of the blinds, where she had spotted it from outside. It pooled in a widening circle just in front of her feet, spreading out from the central point.

He had broken his pattern this time. Not because he hadn't used the machete. He had used that, brought it down in three savage strokes that she could see even from here, the same tell-tale marks as all of the other bodies. But he had stopped there. He had left Shelley's head where it had fallen, tilted back at a grotesque angle from her body, the eyes still wide open with fear, the mouth and skin spattered with her own blood, even now congealing on strands of her hair.

Those wide open eyes stared back at Zoe, meeting her gaze. It was all she could see. The eyes of her partner, open and accusatory, already free of that vital spark that was life. Dead and empty.

Zoe couldn't move. She stood there, the widening pool of blood slowly inching toward her feet, looking into Shelley's dead eyes, the rest of the world gone into a black hole of oblivion that stubbornly refused to take her as well.

Chapter Twenty Two

Zoe sat on the edge of an ambulance's tailgate, shivering in the sun. She couldn't tear her eyes away from Shelley's motel room door, a gaping wide mouth that kept swallowing cops and paramedics and the sheriff and then spitting them out again. Someone had vomited just outside the threshold. She couldn't remember if it was herself or not. Her mouth tasted like ash, either way.

It was like the buzzing of flies over blood. There was a hubbub and a more organized chaos to the buzzing for a moment, and then two paramedics exited the room with a stretcher between them. It was covered with a black bag. Zoe averted her eyes, the only moment that she had been able to. She had already seen enough. She didn't want to see Shelley like that again, not wrapped up in a black bag, not empty of life.

"Listen, Zoe, I'm going to need you to wrap up in this, all right?" someone said, close to her ear. She couldn't understand what their words meant. They were all English, surely, but putting them together made little sense. Something was draped around her shoulders, something that rustled and reflected back bright light into her eyes when she glanced down.

She looked up again, into the gaping maw of the room. It was dark inside there despite all of the sun, and people were milling around still, even more so now that Shelley was gone. They were blocks of color only, green and beige, black, dark blue. Zoe couldn't make out their faces. They were swirling around her like buzzing flies, and she alone stayed still.

Someone was saying something else to her, but she couldn't hear it. She was watching the coroner—she knew it was the coroner from the uniform—talking to the sheriff in the doorway. They both glanced her way. Their faces were blank, empty spaces that she couldn't fill or read.

"Agent." It was the sheriff now, crouching down in front of her. When did he move there? "Zoe. Listen to me, now. We're going to bring you into protective custody, for the moment at least. We need to figure out our next steps. We don't want you to be in any danger, so you're going to have to come with me for a while."

Zoe stared at him. She guessed she was supposed to say something, but she couldn't think. Protective custody? Why did that matter? Shelley was already dead. There was nothing they could do to protect her now.

"The bathroom window was jimmied open," the sheriff continued. "Looks like the suspect fled that way. You wouldn't have been able to see a thing. This isn't your fault."

His hand was on Zoe's shoulder. She stared ahead, lost in her own inner dialogue. What did it matter whose fault it was? The end result was the same.

Zoe doubted that it would matter to Harry whose fault it was that his wife was dead. She was dead either way.

Or Amelia. It probably didn't matter at all to that little girl exactly why her mother wasn't coming home. The result was the same.

Shelley had been a good person. The best of them. Kind and supportive and beautiful. The kind of person who deserved a Hollywood happy ever after ending, with her handsome husband and wonderful daughter, the camera fading to black on happy smiles around the dinner table. She wasn't supposed to end up like this. Dead, empty eyes staring up accusingly above a bloodied neck.

No one deserved to end up like that, but least of all Shelley.

Zoe closed her eyes, no longer wanting to see. The sheriff was guiding her, helping her stand, pulling her over to a car and nudging her to sit down. Zoe turned off her senses, all of them, existing only in the black void inside of her own head. She could see Amelia in there, from the time she had visited Shelley at home. Her little daughter, so full of life and character already, running to embrace her mother.

She saw Harry, too. The way he looked at his wife on their double dinner date. The love and admiration that shone from him. The support he gave her. All of that had been taken away.

That little family had lost everything.

And despite what the sheriff had said, Zoe knew deep in her bones that she would never allow anyone to convince her that it wasn't her fault.

⚜   ⚜   ⚜

Zoe rested her head on her hands, trying to look only at the floor. Maybe it would be quieter there. But even as she stared dead ahead, she saw them all around: measurements of the carpet tiles, the way the gap between them differed by 0.0001 of a millimeter from one to another, the circumference and diameter of certain questionable stains.

She closed her eyes entirely, hoping that would give her some peace. But behind her fingers she knew what was out there: the chaos of the room in the sheriff's station where they had put her, the desks and chairs and computers and posters and files all around her, all of them telling her too much information: length, width, height, relationship, angles, distance, spread, number of pages, and on and on and on. Worse still were the guards the sheriff has positioned with her. Two of his men. She had forgotten their names long ago. They stood by the door and the window, far from silent sentinels, chattering endlessly.

Just seeing them would have been bad enough. Their bodies with all of the calculations they inspired, from the grand to the minute. The way the angles changed every single time they shifted their weight or moved their hands. But the conversation was the worst part. She counted words per sentence, syllables, vowels, consonants, slang terms, pentameter, rhythm, the length of their pauses. All of it battled for her attention, never giving her a single moment of rest.

Zoe wanted to cry. Wanted to scream and tell everything to shut up, just shut up, stop *being*, stop distracting her. But that wouldn't help anything. It would only make them look at her with pity and revulsion. She wasn't stupid. She'd been here before.

And through it all, like the chord progression backing the vocals and percussion of life around her, was a refrain she could not break away from. Three strokes to sever the neck. Five-centimeter dent in the skull. Two pints of blood on the walls and other objects in the room alone. Two wide, glassy eyes. A distance of a third of a foot between the head and the body. Over and over again, the scene repeated in her head.

Zoe pressed the cell phone to her ear, wondering if the call would at least help to drown something out.

"...Zoe?" She dimly became aware that the voice might have been talking to her for some time, and that she hadn't answered. She glanced up at the two guards who had positioned with her. Either they recognized the urgency of the situation and shut up to give her peace, or the look she gave them terrified them into silence. She didn't feel it mattered particularly which.

"Sir?" she replied, fighting her way through the exhaustion of the numbers to answer him.

"Good, I thought I'd lost you for a moment," SAIC Maitland said. Had she called him? Or did he call her? Zoe couldn't remember. Everything was moving in a strange kind of way, like she was trapped outside of time and yet also losing huge chunks of it. "Did you hear what I said? We've rebooked the flight. You'll be on your way home in a couple of hours."

Something about that wasn't quite right, though Zoe couldn't figure out what. "Way home," she repeated numbly.

"Yes. As soon as possible. I'm sending in a team of agents to take over the case—it's clear this is a serious investigation that requires more manpower. I don't want you to feel that you have to shoulder the responsibility anymore. It's over. You need to come home and recover."

"Come home," Zoe repeated, having finally grasped what about it didn't makes sense. "Without her."

There was a pause. Maitland sighed, his breath noisy down the line. Zoe counted the length of his exhale. Four seconds. "I know this is difficult," he said. "Losing an agent in the line of duty always is. The two of you were doing everything right. You had the most likely suspect locked away. No one could have foreseen this."

"He came for her," Zoe whispered. "Why not for me?"

Maitland cleared his throat loudly, and even so, when he spoke there was something of a fracture in his voice, a line that threatened to divide him. "You can't blame yourself for this, Agent Prime. It could just have easily been you, and I don't know if that's a comfort or not. The most obvious conclusion would have to be that the killer saw your press conference on the news. I'm sure he simply targeted Michelle because he recognized her from there. He was likely trying to stop us from digging any further—perhaps he thought that she had discovered something incriminating..."

Zoe frowned. It was so hard to hold onto the meaning of what he was saying. Instead, she knew that he had spoken seventy-two words, the longest of them five syllables long. But something had caught at her attention, like a rock snagging a piece of fabric. Something jagged and sharp and wrong.

"Michelle?" she asked. Who was he talking about? Michelle Young, the other victim? What did he mean by linking back to that case?

"Agent Rose," Maitland replied. "Shelley, as I believe she liked to be called."

Something thudded deep and heavy in Zoe's chest. Michelle. Shelley's real name was Michelle. How had she not realized that?

They had been close. Not just colleagues and partners, but friends. Shelley had invited Zoe to her home. They had been out to dinner with their other halves, all four of them together. They had been friends. By every metric Zoe knew how to analyze, they were friends.

How could she not have known that Shelley wasn't even her full name?

Zoe heard nothing else that Maitland said to her. She threw in a "yes, sir" whenever it seemed appropriate, mechanically answering him, as if she was a robot programmed to respond to humans and not the real thing herself. She ended the call when he did, dropping the cell phone down into her lap and staring at her hands, mostly because she did not want to stare at anything else.

Michelle Rose. The name sounded alien to her. The name of someone else, someone she had never known. All of the pieces of the things she thought she had known were turning to sand and tumbling through her fingers, spilling to the floor with the remnants of everything else.

CHAPTER TWENTY THREE

Z oe stared at the digital ticket on the screen, seeing the codes and numbers but making no sense of them. Her flight had been booked again. Just one seat this time. No one to sit next to her, to talk to her on the journey, to offer companionable silence. Just one ticket.

"The other agents will be here a few hours after you leave," the sheriff was saying. "Agents Ambrose and Ziltsman. You know them?"

Zoe shook her head dumbly. Other agents? What did she care about other agents? Right now there was only one agent who mattered, and she wasn't going to be coming back to work on the case any time soon. She wasn't going to be coming back, ever.

"Anyway, they'll take over on the case. So you don't need to worry about anything, all right?" There was something fatherly about Sheriff Hawthorne's manner, but nothing was hitting Zoe. It was like there was a shield up in front of her, and nothing good or kind could get through. Maybe it was a shield of her own devising. She deserved that. "Just leave it to us now. We'll figure out who took your partner's life and bring him to justice. I promise you that."

It wasn't right. Zoe shook her head, feeling an echo of pain in her skull, the headache intensifying with the movement. "I can't leave it to anyone," she said. "It's Shelley. I have to do this for her. I have to stop him."

"You won't be able to do anything from home," the sheriff said, not unreasonably. "It's better that you get some rest. Shelley would have wanted that for you. Take care of yourself. Go back home to the people you love."

The people she loved? Zoe knew, even as he said it, that it wasn't possible. Shelley had been one of those people. Even if Zoe hadn't known her as well as she thought, it was undeniable that she had let Shelley in further than almost anyone. There were two people in her life who knew her secret. That said something.

"Then I won't go home," Zoe said, which seemed to be the best way to combat the obstacle he had pointed out. Staying here would mean that she was able to keep working on the case. That was the obvious solution.

The sheriff sighed. "You look exhausted. Perhaps you can try and get some rest before the flight. We've got your things from the motel and we'll escort you to the airport when the time comes. I can give you an empty conference room if you'd like, somewhere to get your head down a bit."

Zoe nodded once, then struggled to her feet and followed the sheriff on legs made of lead down the hall. He showed her into the empty room, which at least had seating and not much else, and hesitated at the door.

"I'll leave McWillard outside the door in case you need anything," he said. "Don't hesitate to ask. But I'll tell him not to disturb you until it's time to go." He paused, and Zoe vaguely thought that he might be waiting for an answer, though he hadn't asked a question. He finally turned and left, and the door clanged shut behind him like the closing of a vault.

Zoe sighed and settled into a chair, feeling the way it seemed to embrace every single ache in her body and make it worse. There was something about the chairs that law enforcement offices always seemed to use, whether they were police precincts or the FBI headquarters themselves. Uncomfortable. Always putting the suspect on edge, stopping them from relaxing. The problem was, the same thing went for the investigators.

Zoe tried to focus her thoughts, but she couldn't seem to get anywhere—let alone remember what she was supposed to be focusing on. Outside the door McWillard was leaning against the wall, talking in a low voice. She couldn't make out his words, only the rhythm and cadence. The sound dug away at her, clawing out numbers as if carving them from her very soul, leaving her raw and bloody.

Zoe shut her eyes. There was nothing else to distract her in here, nothing but McWillard and his stupid voice. She tried to concentrate. Maybe if she could try the techniques that her therapist, Dr. Monk, had suggested . . . She started counting her breaths, in and then out for one, in and then out for two. In and then out for—and the rhythm of his voice was a pattern she could almost identify, a cadence that was very particular, a one-two one one-two, one one one, one-two.

Dammit—she knew she had slipped away from the meditation, the breaths. She started again. In and out for one. Maybe just breathing wouldn't be enough. She needed to go to her island, the private tropical island in her head where everything was quiet and calm, and no one distracted her. Where the numbers couldn't reach and a palm tree was just a palm tree, not a series of measurements and calculations.

She couldn't even get past the breathing exercise to lead her to the island, let alone reach the shore.

Zoe got up and banged heavily on the door. "Shut up!" she yelled. She didn't care how it sounded. She was suffering here. Couldn't he see that?

There was a shuffling sound, someone's weight being moved around on the surface of the door itself. A murmuring of the voice she recognized, two syllables. Perhaps a quiet apology.

Zoe sunk back into her chair, putting her head in her hands once again. In and out for one, in the silence. In and out for two.

She reached ten and opened her eyes—not her real eyes, but the eyes inside her head—to see the familiar tranquil island close by. She bobbed on a gentle current, letting it sway her closer to the sand under a bright blue sky. The sun beat down on her skin. She looked toward a familiar stand of trees where there should have been a hammock, where sometimes John swung lazily, but he was not there. No one was there. There was no hammock.

Zoe looked down at the water, and saw with a start that it was the color of blood.

She opened her eyes—her real eyes—and shot up from her chair, beginning to pace up and down the room. There was no refuge on her island. Nor did she deserve it. Shelley was dead. This wasn't a time to be relaxing and dreaming of piña coladas and bikini weather.

She was going about this all wrong. The numbers weren't an enemy to wrestle with and beat down. They were the thing that would save her. That should have saved Shelley. If she had just stopped repressing them and tried to see, to really *see*, then maybe this case would have been over already. Maybe Shelley would be alive. Maybe Zoe would never have made the mistake of thinking that some bitter old pervert could possibly be responsible for a string of gruesome murders, all of which targeted young women with a vicious ferocity tied by strange calm.

The young women—and now Shelley one of them. She was the right age group, even. And all because she was investigating the case.

But it was such a coincidence, wasn't it? There had to be something about Shelley that made the killer think she knew something more than Zoe did, or else they would both be dead. And why take that risk? Eliminate one to stall the investigation, and yet leave the other one alive and still able to lead the case? It didn't make sense.

It didn't make sense at all, no matter how she twisted and turned it. Why kill someone to divert suspicion, anyway? The suspicion had already been diverted. They had a suspect in custody. They could quite happily have spent the next few years taking Dr. Edgerton to trial, and even if he was eventually found innocent, the trail by then would have run cold. Whoever the killer really was, he would have had years to get away with it: to move states, to flee to Brazil, to get a new identity and start again.

So, why? Why come forward now and kill again, when you were just about to get away with it scot-free? Not only that, but to kill an FBI agent—the kind of victim that law enforcement would never allow to go unavenged. Cop killers didn't evade justice. They were hounded down doggedly, for years if that's what it took, because the investigators involved had that personal connection that meant they would never give up until someone was behind bars. Or in the ground. Whatever it took.

There had to be some reason why the killer wouldn't just let the doctor take the fall for his misdeeds. Pride was often a personality flaw in these serial cases. There were those killers who secretly wanted credit, praise, to be famous for what they had done. Or else those who wanted to be caught, left as many clues behind as they could, so that the police could stop them from killing again.

And yet the suspect so far had been so careful. Not a single piece of evidence left to identify him until the Ivy Griffiths case, and that was just a shoeprint. Someone that careful didn't want to be caught. They wanted to get away with it forever. They wanted to be free so that they could kill again.

Was that it? Just simple bloodlust? An insatiable need to take life that couldn't be stopped, even if it meant saving the killer's own skin? But then, again, Zoe came back around on herself. If that was the case, why go after just about the most high-profile target you could get, as far as the FBI was concerned? Why not some anonymous housewife, or a loner who wouldn't be missed for days or weeks as the investigation stalled on a false suspect?

Why Shelley?

Michelle. She remembered her earlier thought, on the phone with Maitland. There were two victims called Michelle now, and that had confused her earlier. If it wasn't for the fact that it was *Shelley*, she probably would have seen it earlier. A correlation. Any repeat in the data wasn't to be dismissed as mere coincidence. It was to be investigated and tested, poked and prodded to see if it could shed any more light on the killer and his motives and methods.

Zoe knew that. Normally it would not have escaped her notice for this long. But she had it now. Two Michelles. Not only that, but there were two blondes in the original suspect pool, and now three with Shelley. Additionally, they were mostly within the same kind of height and build parameters, without being all precisely the same. There was a picturing beginning to emerge. A young woman, around average to below average height, a slim build, blonde hair. A Michelle.

The data was there, but what did it mean? Zoe tried to think harder. Knowing what the next victim might look like wasn't particularly helpful. There were definitely too many Michelles in Nebraska to be able to place them all under protective surveillance, let alone the amount of women who would be blonde and the right figure. It was too vague. The data points were clear, but unhelpful.

Seeing through the killer's eyes and identifying his perfect victim meant nothing to her. She couldn't see how he thought and get anything helpful from it.

So, whose eyes did she need to see through?

How would Shelley see it?

Zoe tried to think like her partner, to shade in colors that were based on emotion rather than numbers. To get the personal connections, the dots that comprised a person that weren't data points. Things you couldn't define in numbers, the kind of things that had always evaded her.

She had a victim profile. But where did the profile come from? If the killer was targeting women of a certain type, then it wasn't coincidence. It wasn't luck. It was design. The killer was seeking an archetype, putting together a picture as if the women were jigsaw pieces in a larger puzzle.

That was it.

There was some original picture here—like the image on the jigsaw box, used as a blueprint for putting the pieces together. You could compare the pieces to the image: see a nose here, a hair color there, even a matching name. But you had to have the picture on the box in order to compare them to. That meant there was a woman—maybe dead, maybe alive—who had been the original.

Zoe went over the data points again. A blonde, mid – to late twenties woman named Michelle, slim build and average to below average height. That was who they needed to look for. Not the killer—the man who had left behind so little evidence that they didn't even know where to start searching for him. But the woman.

Somewhere out there was a Michelle who was the key to unlocking the whole case, whether she knew it or not. And Zoe knew she wasn't going to be able to get on a plane until she found her.

Chapter Twenty Four

"Sir," Zoe said resolutely. "I insist."

"Agent Prime, you're in shock," Maitland said, his voice taking on a terser tone. "You've been ordered to return home. The ticket is booked and paid for. I have agents preparing to come to the airport over here. You don't need to remain on this case."

"I know I do not need to," Zoe told him, pacing up and down with the cell phone pressed to her ear, seven steps each way. "I want to. I am not in shock anymore. I know this case better than the others will. I already have all of the information. I have a lead. I need to follow it."

"I do not approve of this," Maitland said, in a tone that brooked no argument. "You need to be back here getting some rest, and getting some help. You'll need to see our therapist for mandated sessions until we know how this trauma has affected you. I have a duty of care—"

"I have a duty," Zoe interrupted him. She had never argued with him before, not like this. Her whole career had been about keeping her head down, trying not to stand out. Making arrests when and where she could without compromising her secret. When she had been in trouble, it had been for things she'd done in service of that goal. She had never butted heads with a superior on purpose, for something she hadn't even done yet—but this time mattered. It mattered more than anything else. "I have a duty to Shelley, and her husband, and her young daughter. You are asking me to get on a plane and turn my back on this whole case, when I have a shot at finding the killer and bringing him in."

There was a long pause. Zoe was about to open her mouth and say something else, fill in even more reasons why she should be allowed to stay, when Maitland finally answered. "Do you know about the five stages of grief, Agent Prime?"

"Of course." It was a numbered list of easily definable items; Zoe liked it.

"It sounds to me like you're entering anger," Maitland said. "Can I even trust you to keep a lid on your emotions right now? To control yourself? What are you going to do if you come across this killer? What if you have him in your sights and there's no one around to see you pull the trigger?"

"I do not want him dead, sir," Zoe told him. It was almost funny, really—someone questioning her on whether she could rein in her emotions. Usually the complaint was the opposite. "I want him in the prison system. He killed an FBI agent. I know how much of a hell his life will be if we get him behind bars."

Maitland blew out a breath, clearly thinking. "That's cold rage, right there," he said. "If I do allow you to stay—and that's a big if—what do you need?"

"Access to the Nebraska state police records, to search for records of previous cases," she said. "I believe the killer is attempting to recreate an archetype in the selection of his victims. Somewhere there will be the first case, the original. At first I thought it might have been Michelle Young, but she was the tallest of them. If she was the archetype, he would be going after tall women, not women who look like Shelley or Ivy Griffiths. There must be another."

Silence on the other side again, as Maitland considered what she had said. "What if you can't find someone in the database who matches those parameters?"

"Then maybe the archetype is still alive, and we can still save her before he works his way up to killing her," Zoe said. "This is not just about my partner. He killed three other women, that we know of. He will kill again. Statistics tell us that he will escalate. If you let new agents take over, there will be a delay as they get up to speed. They will need to retread old ground that I have already covered. I have been present at two of the live crime scenes. Sir, it needs to be me."

There was a muffled noise, as if Maitland had covered his face with his hand and brushed against the receiver. "All right," he groaned. "I can already feel myself regretting this, but stay there. I'll organize access to the records for you. Agent Prime, please, let's end this case with me being pleasantly surprised by how much control you managed to exert over yourself, yes?"

"Yes, sir," Zoe said, ending the call before he had the chance to change his mind.

✤ ✤ ✤

Zoe jumped out of the car outside the police precinct, barely pausing to turn off the engine as she did so. There was a fire inside of her that would not allow her to sit still or go slow. She needed answers, and she needed them now.

"Hey," she said, flashing her FBI badge at the startled officer behind the desk. She was a mousey thing, almost too short to meet state regulations on height, Zoe saw. "I need access to your records."

"Oh," the officer stammered. "Er, do we have—have you got—I mean, you'd need permission to access..."

Zoe looked around impatiently, trying to find a sign or some indication of which direction to go in. "Your chief should have received a communication via email from Special Agent in Charge Maitland at the J. Edgar Hoover Building. This is urgent. Which way is his office?"

"Oh, gosh, just let me give him a call," the officer said in alarm, but Zoe was already heading by her, trying doors on the right-hand side of the desk. "Ma'am, those are all locked for keycard access only, if you'll just give me a minute..."

"Buzz me in," Zoe told her.

"Er, I don't..."

"Buzz me in."

The officer swallowed nervously, then reached down to push a button under her desk. The door made an electrical whirring sound, and then clicked open. Zoe pushed through, marching down the corridor in search of anyone who looked as though they had enough authority to give her access to the files she needed, ignoring three unmarked doors.

She already knew that she was onto something. She had accessed NCIC from the sheriff's station—the national database that all law enforcement agencies were supposed to use in order to enter details of their crimes and the salient information that might connect them to other cases, or help get them solved.

There, she had found a potential hit. A local case of a missing person, although the report was only half-complete with much of the important information missing. It was listed as having been entered by this precinct; given how close she was, she didn't want to sit and wait for someone to answer her call and go through files whenever it suited them to eventually email her a few extra points. She wanted the data right from the source, and she wanted it before the day was over.

"Excuse me?" A man stepped forward from around the corner in a dark uniform, several badges on his chest and shoulders marking him out as someone of higher status. "Can I help you?"

"Are you the captain here?" Zoe asked.

"Yes, I'm Captain Tarroway. Why are you wandering about back here without an escort?"

Zoe had no time to be insulted at his tone. She was only impatient. She grabbed out her badge again and held it in his face. "Special Agent Zoe Prime. If you have been reading your emails, you should be expecting me."

The man, who was around forty-five years old and six feet tall with thick eyebrows, blinked. "You're the agent coming to check our files? That was . . . fast. I wasn't expecting you until tomorrow at least."

"I am here now," Zoe said. There was no time for pleasantries or explanations. "Show me to the records."

The captain looked about to say something else, but then he wet his lips nervously and turned on his heel. "Follow me," he said.

He led her to a records room down in the basement, which was musty and damp. Brown boxes filled with files sat on metal cabinets across the length and breadth of the room, with only a couple of feet provided for aisles between them. Zoe made a quick estimate based on what she could see: perhaps six hundred boxes altogether. A set of cages along one side of the room served as an evidence locker, with guns, bags of powdery substances, and bloodied clothing visible through the mesh.

"This is where we keep our closed or cold cases," he said. "The details should be somewhere in here. I think the email said something about missing persons?"

"That is correct," Zoe told him. "I am looking into a very particular case. The NCIC entry was not complete. It was a woman who went missing three months and two weeks ago. Her married name is Michelle Hastie; she may also be listed under her maiden name, as Michelle Griffiths."

The revelation of the name in the case record had been startling, a slap in the face. The same surname as the victim, Ivy Griffiths. They had not been related—at least, not that Zoe could see. Being both in the same state, it was possible that they were cousins of a magnitude of removal that meant they had never been aware of one another. But it was a common name. Equally likely that they shared no blood at all.

"Right," the captain muttered. "And do you have a case file number from the listing?"

Zoe rattled it off easily, memorized in a matter of seconds as she had browsed it on Sheriff Hawthorne's ancient computer. She followed the captain as he moved between the racks, navigating with a hesitant step as he traced case numbers on boxes and followed them toward their target. He clearly was not used to moving around down here; Zoe would have guessed that he normally had less senior officers take care of the filing. She had figured out the pattern of the numbers and was aching to move ahead of him before he found it.

"Ah, here we are," he announced, pulling out a slim file. Zoe's heart sank, just a little. It was still possible that it held salient information. "As I recall, there wasn't a lot to go on with this one. You may have your work cut out for you. Or is it that you think you've found her already?"

"It's an ongoing murder investigation," Zoe told him, snatching the folder out of his hands and already turning away. There were three pages in the folder. She would have hoped for more. It was possible that the information entered into NCIC was all they had to go on and it had been entered into the system correctly after all. She gauged weight, hoping against hope that she was wrong.

There was a low counter near the door, the top of a refrigeration unit that would serve just as well as a table. Zoe spread the file open on top of it, squinting in the dim light, leafing through the three pages to see what they could tell her. Her eyes skimmed over the first page: Michelle Hastie alias Michelle Griffiths, five foot six, twenty-six years old, one hundred and twenty pounds. Last known address, associates, ex-husband, reported missing by a colleague, place of work. The next page was a description of her home and its contents: everything still there except for a single suitcase, a few empty hangers. Passport and purse missing. On the face of it, it seemed quite plausible that she had simply gotten fed up or scared or something else and decided to skip town.

Zoe flipped to the last page. It was a statement from the colleague, the one who had made the report, about Michelle and her habits, and how disappearing out of the blue was unusual for her. That was mostly uninteresting, but what was very interesting indeed was the addition of a single photographic print in the file.

Zoe held it up, catching the light that filtered down from behind one of the evidence stacks. Michelle Hastie was a blonde woman with a fresh face and dainty features. She was not pictured in full in the image—only her head and torso—but Zoe could easily see that the height and weight figures provided were likely to be accurate. Her heart lurched in her chest. In this photograph she could see little snippets of all of them: Ivy Griffiths's figure, the eyes and mouth of Lorna Troye, Michelle Young's neatness—and the pretty, cheerful, friendly disposition of Shelley Rose.

Zoe caught herself staring at the photograph with her mouth open and hastily put it down, turning back to the captain, whose name she had already forgotten. "There's no report on the progress made by your officers," she said.

"Then there was none." The captain shrugged. He had been reading over her shoulder. "A missing person, it's usually nothing. Something like this where she took her money and clothes, we wouldn't have prioritized it over other cases. Looks like she just ran away. That happens sometimes."

"She didn't just run away," Zoe said. "What about interviews? Surely your officers spoke to people in her life—suspects—her landlord—anyone who could shed some light on her disappearance?"

The captain made a humming noise, then turned to the first page again. An officer's name was listed there as the man in charge of the search. "Let's go upstairs and talk to Sergeant Daison. He will have conducted them."

Zoe trailed him up the set of twelve stairs, feeling frustrated and itchy, needing to get on with the action. Numbers were buzzing around here: the length and height of each step, the wear on the captain's shoes in front of her and the variation in millimeters between the left and the right, the number of marks on the wall.

The disappearance of women treated as nothing out of the ordinary: she had come across it time and time again. Whether it was a young teen forced into prostitution who was categorized as a rebellious runaway, or an indigenous wife who slipped through the cracks because it was deemed tribal business, there were altogether too many cases of this ilk.

And if they were killed, almost every time you could guarantee that it would be linked to another cold case, or a recent murder. Almost every time, the thrill of doing it and getting away with it tempted the killer to strike again. These were patterns that were easily identifiable. The statistics were clear. If she'd had the time and wasn't chasing down the most important case she had ever worked on, Zoe might have taken a while to educate the locals on why it was important to follow up every single time—even when it looked innocent.

As they returned to the empty hall but then emerged out into the noisy bullpen, Zoe felt the world hemming in around her. There were ten desks scattered with paperwork and tchotchkes, framed photographs, lunchboxes. Several officers were sitting behind them or milling around, and behind them all was a larger office that must have belonged to the captain. She could barely concentrate: their heights, the distance between desks, the number of items in each area and their respective measurements...

"Sarge," the captain said, pausing at a desk that was set at the top of the bullpen. The man behind it was tall and imposing, narrow as a rake. Six foot three easily, though he was currently seated. Zoe tried to force herself to stop counting the inches of collar at the neck of his shirt and focus on the conversation. "This is Special Agent Prime of the FBI. She's looking into one of your cold cases. Have you got witness statements? Missing person, Michelle Hastie."

Sergeant Daison blinked and nodded, beginning to rifle through sheets of paper on his desk. "I keep them up here," he said. "I know it's technically a cold case, but something never sat right with me on that one. I keep an eye on the people involved when I can."

It was Zoe's turn to blink. She had misinterpreted the lack of completeness in entering the data or filing the report as lack of care. On the contrary, the pages that Sergeant Daison pulled out were worn and wrinkled at the edges from frequent thumbing, and judging by the huge number of files piled around the rest of his desk, he was too busy a man to finish an online report for a case that he still thought of as active.

"If you'd talk Agent Prime through it," the captain said, his voice distant as he had already turned away toward his office. "I'll be inside if you need me."

"Do you think you've found her?" Daison asked, looking up at Zoe expectantly.

"No," she said, clearing her throat and tearing her eyes away from the retreating captain's back, where she had been examining the measurements of his suit. "Unfortunately. I'm covering a string of murders. Beheadings."

Daison's eyes widened. "I've been following the case on the news. They all look like her."

"Yes," Zoe confirmed. She was glad that the news coverage had not yet begun to report on Shelley's death. She wanted to avoid awkward platitudes as much as possible.

"We never found Michelle," Daison said, handing her the pages. "I conducted interviews with everyone in her life I could get ahold of. To me, it was too perfect a staging. Only a few clothes and the essentials you would always think to check taken. But there was jewelry left behind—pieces that would have been worth something to sell. Underwear. A laptop. The kind of things you would pack if you weren't planning on ever coming back."

"The file noted she was recently divorced," Zoe said. She couldn't both read the pages and talk to Daison at the same time, so she let him tell it in his own words. Knowing that he cared now, she had a newfound respect for his opinion.

"Yeah, husband was this guy, Paul Hastie. I interviewed him right after the report was made. He said that he hadn't seen Michelle in months, since she first served him with divorce papers. It had gone through by then, although Michelle hadn't gotten around to changing her name."

"Did you believe him?"

Daison made a face. "It's tough. I wondered about him. It's always someone she knows, you know? Nine times out of ten. Ex-husband would normally be a shoo-in. But he was with a new girlfriend already. She verified they'd been staying together that weekend, out of town. Lovers' getaway. Hours away. No chance of him being able to slip out without her, she said. I asked about when she was asleep, and she told me they didn't get much sleeping done. That kind of trip."

Zoe narrowed her eyes, thinking as she tapped her notebook against the papers that Daison had shown her. "You believe her?"

"Yeah, I think so. She's a sweet thing. Wouldn't hurt a fly, was my impression. Real shocked to hear about Michelle going missing. Concerned."

"Motives for Michelle to disappear through her own choice?"

Daison shrugged. "Couldn't find any. Ex-husband said something about her having a fantasy of running away to . . . where was it . . ." He consulted his notes, flipping to the second page of the interview transcription. "Yeah, here. Puerto Rico. He was the only one that gave me that, so I don't know how much I trust it. Bit too convenient."

"Hmm." Zoe glanced over the pages properly, skimming words from the text. She was more thinking than reading. "Do you have a current address for this girlfriend?"

"Yeah." Daison turned to his computer and made a few taps. "I have it right here. She's in town. Her name is Victoria Lee." He scrawled it out quickly on a Post-it and handed it over.

Zoe nodded her thanks at him as she took pictures of the interview reports with her phone. She could read them later. "Tell your captain I left," she said, having no desire to interact further with the man herself. She crossed the bull-pen unsteadily, dodging noise and officers with paperwork and one perp in cuffs, trying not to give away how sick the chaotic atmosphere made her feel.

Out in the corridor she gasped for air, then made her way back to reception. There was no time to sit around feeling sorry for herself. Not while Shelley's killer was still on the loose.

Chapter Twenty Five

Zoe rapped hard on the door, standing back a step to look up and down the street one more time. It was a normal, rather boring suburban neighborhood: the houses here were modest, but well-kept. Starter homes for people who cared about where they lived.

She had a rage boiling in her blood, a purpose that would not be quelled by anything. The numbers were glancing off her eyes like sparks, only fueling the flames. The walk from the car to the front door was four feet. Each step burned higher in Zoe's body, making her straighten her shoulders, sharpening her gaze. She would have her answers. Whoever this girlfriend was, she was going to tell Zoe everything she knew about Michelle Hastie—and everything she knew about her killer.

The door opened and a petite young woman with pretty Asian features glanced up at Zoe. She had a carefree smile on her face which quickly drifted into confusion at not knowing who it was that was there to see her. She *was* small and sweet-looking, like Sergeant Daison had said. Zoe almost faltered, but she pushed on. Overlaid on what she saw in front of her was Shelley's dead eyes, open and staring.

"Victoria Lee?" Zoe snapped out, before the woman had a chance to speak.

She nodded uncertainly.

"I am Special Agent Zoe Prime," Zoe said, flashing her badge. "I would like to come in and ask you some questions."

The way she said it—flat and straight—left no room for argument. Victoria faltered, then nodded, stepping aside to allow Zoe in.

Zoe walked straight through to the living room, identifying it through years of knowledge of the pattern in which homes were normally built and a bit of luck. She wasn't willing to stop or slow down. A fire was burning in her head, a fire that had Shelley's name as the fuel. She was close now: she could feel it. And if this little Asian-American woman was the key to stopping Shelley's killer, then Zoe was going to twist her until the whole thing was unlocked, sweet nature or not.

"C-can I get you anything?" Victoria stammered. She hovered in the doorway as Zoe chose a chair on the opposite side of the room, facing a television, and sat down. "Coffee or tea?"

"No," Zoe said shortly. She was analyzing Victoria, analyzing the room, all of it. She was five two, maybe a hundred pounds wringing wet, small and compact. Her hair was cut in a straight line just at her shoulders, her lips a perfect bow, her face almost exactly symmetrical. She had wide eyes rimmed with just a touch of mascara, blinking up at Zoe now with total confusion and anxiety. "Sit down, Victoria."

Victoria sat, folding herself onto a sofa that dwarfed her, tucking her hands neatly into her lap. Her straight eyebrows, which appeared to be naturally shaped, made a T-shape against the center line of her nose. She was all angles and lines, and yet there was something soft about the overall impression she gave.

"What's this about?" she asked, her voice thin and musical.

Zoe blinked away the measurements and patterns, reminding herself to try to look past them and see *Victoria* instead. "A few months ago, you were questioned in connection with the disappearance of a local woman. Michelle Hastie."

"Oh!" Victoria's eyes lit up. "Paul's ex-wife. Have you found her? Is she safe? Paul always said she was just having a good time in Puerto Rico."

"No," Zoe said. She was watching Victoria carefully. This was not entirely what she had been waiting for. "We have not found her."

The girl deflated like a balloon, her shoulders sagging. Her doll-like face drifted down, the corners of her lips tweaking toward the floor. "That's a shame. We've been wondering, all this time. I haven't been able to put her out of my mind. I just keep hoping that she's all right."

Zoe narrowed her eyes. The reaction wasn't what she had been expecting—the opposite, even. Relief, perhaps, that the crime had not been discovered. Guilt. But there was only what looked to Zoe, at least, like genuine concern and regret. "Are you still in a relationship with Paul?"

"Yes," Victoria said, a shy smile lighting her face up again. "It's been about six months now."

"Where do you think he will be at the moment?" She hadn't planned this line of questioning, exactly. In fact, she had been planning to force a confession, no matter what it took. But this girl was timid and sweet, and her heart was written all over her face. She genuinely thought there was a chance Michelle was still alive, genuinely hoped for it. She had no idea that she was dating a murderer.

Because that was what he was. Zoe had little doubt about that now. The disappearance of his ex-wife so close to all of these murders of women who looked just like her—there was no longer any way that he looked innocent. She had come to Victoria hoping for a sign of guilt, a confrontation, an excuse to slap someone in handcuffs and drag them away. She wasn't going to get it. Victoria knew nothing. She was totally in love. That much was obvious even to Zoe, from the basic facts she knew about body language angles and patterns and what the lines of the face revealed about thought.

"He's at work," Victoria told her, her fingers fluttering nervously together. She was unsure about whether to reach for her cell phone, sitting on the arm of the sofa. Zoe counted the beats of her digits: seven, twelve, fifteen.

"What does Paul do now, Victoria?"

"He's an insurance appraiser. He—he travels all over this and the next few counties for work, so he might be anywhere. Why do you need to speak to him?"

"It is regarding his ex-wife. Does he have a central office?"

"Yes, it's . . ." Victoria hesitated. She was unsettled now, unsure of how much she should tell. How much would be a betrayal of Paul's trust.

"Give me the address," Zoe said. "I can find it out anyway. Better that it comes from you now and quickly. I do not want to have to arrest you for obstruction of justice."

Victoria gasped, her breath catching in her throat as her face paled. "Is Paul in trouble?" she asked, her voice wispy and quiet.

"That depends on what he tells me." Zoe paused, taking in Victoria's appearance. She was visibly trembling. Her hand kept straying to a small heart pendant that hung around her throat. Probably a gift from Paul. She was loyal, in love, blind to what he was truly like. She needed to know. "Victoria, listen to me closely. Paul is not the man that you think he is. He is dangerous. I am investigating him in connection with a string of murders of young women, starting with his ex-wife."

Victoria continued to stare at her with wide eyes, her lips parted. She was breathing shallowly, moisture beginning to glisten at the edges of her lids. "That's...that's not..."

"Paul is dangerous," Zoe repeated. "Believe me when I say that I have no shadow of a doubt that he is a violent killer. He took the life of my partner earlier today. All of the killings link back to Michelle. Do you understand what I am saying?"

"Y...yes..." Victoria screwed her eyes shut. "No. Paul's lovely. He's gentle. He wouldn't..."

"He would," Zoe told her. "History is littered with killers who looked normal and harmless at home. Believe what I am saying. Your own safety relies on it. Do not contact him. Do not tell him we spoke. Do not reach out to ask him if it is true. He may come back here and attempt to harm you."

Victoria was leaning forward slightly, clutching at her own knees for stability. She was still gasping for breath, and fat tears were beginning to slide down her cheeks. "But he's supposed to be coming over here after work."

Good. A chance to catch him later, if she couldn't find him at work. Zoe would be able to tell the local PD, the sheriff, give them a chance to convene on the house and wait for him. "If he comes early, you must pretend that nothing is wrong. Do you understand? Do not let on that you know. Get some distance from him—go into the bathroom, maybe, and contact me immediately." She took a business card out of her inside pocket and slid it across the neat coffee table between them. It was decorated with two pink ceramic bowls, containing seven items of fresh fruit and two decorative candles that smelled, even while unlit, faintly of strawberries.

Victoria took the card, studying it blindly in that way that people had who were totally overwhelmed, and nodded. "O-okay. I'll call you if he comes back."

"Victoria." Zoe said the word hard enough that the girl looked up, her attention back on Zoe. "Do not let him know that you know. It is extremely important that he thinks everything is fine. You will only have to stall him until I arrive with the local police. He will not hurt you if he does not know the net is closing in."

Victoria nodded one more time, reaching up to scrub at her cheeks. A thin trail of mascara hung under her eyes. "I'll try to act normal," she said, sniffing and blinking, forcing back more tears.

It wasn't particularly convincing, but Zoe had no time to stop and be a shoulder for Victoria to cry on. She had to go. Him coming back here was not the best-case scenario. She had to catch him at work—before he even suspected anything was up.

"Now," she said. "That address?"

CHAPTER TWENTY SIX

Zoe pulled up alongside the sidewalk with a scream of her wheels and jumped out of the car, almost knocking over a pedestrian as she whirled past them. The insurance firm was housed in a large gray building, almost blending with the sidewalk itself, a flat expanse of concrete stretching up above the street. There were large glass windows on every floor.

Zoe sprinted inside and headed straight for the reception area, where a fifty-two-year-old woman in a sharp gray skirt suit stood behind a desk that was entirely composed of both clear and frosted glass. She took out her badge and slammed it, open, on top of the desk without bothering to introduce herself. "Paul Hastie," she said. "Where is he?"

The receptionist blinked behind half-moon glasses. "Excuse me?"

"I said," Zoe began, but the receptionist was already cutting her off.

"I can't just give out the whereabouts of our employees," she said.

Zoe had had enough of being given the run-around or having to stand on ceremony. There was no time for this—this stupid woman was just standing in her way. In her head seconds ticked out distractingly—*eighteen, nineteen* . . . "This badge says you can," she hissed through gritted teeth. "Paul Hastie. Now."

The receptionist began to reach for the cordless phone on her desk, but Zoe reached out and grabbed hold of her arm with a viselike grip. "No warning him. Is he here, or not?"

The receptionist licked her lips carefully. She kept glancing down at her arm. Zoe let go when she began to withdraw. "I can check the online schedule," she said tentatively. "Other than calling him on his direct line, I can't be absolutely sure."

"Check it," Zoe ordered. She glanced around the reception area behind her. There were two people sitting stiffly on chairs, watching her with alarm:

civilians. She dismissed them immediately. Of more immediate concern was a man inching back through a doorway beside them, dressed in a suit the precise same shade of gray as the receptionist. The uniform reduced him to a statistic. Employee number two.

"You," Zoe said, pointing at him. "Stay where you are. I will not risk him knowing I am coming for him."

"What's he done?" the employee asked, almost under his breath.

What, Zoe thought. The man wasn't surprised to hear that Paul was in trouble. Didn't deny that anything could possibly be wrong. That was something.

"He's not in the office at the moment," the receptionist said, her words tripping just a bit too quickly. Zoe was about to question her out of disbelief, but when she marked the woman's more relaxed posture, she realized it was relief, not a lie, that made her rush. "He's out on an assessment."

"Where?" Zoe demanded. She pushed her notebook toward the woman, open on a blank page. "Give me the address."

"Should we be worried?" the employee behind her asked.

"No," Zoe said, even though they should, because it was quicker than explaining everything. "But if he comes back, don't tell him I was looking for him. Just call me and let me know. It's essential he doesn't know I was here." She slipped another business card over the counter. Her last one. It had been a busy trip.

There was no time to stop and wait to see if they understood and would really do as she asked. People were too tricky, too slippery. Zoe had never been good at telling truth from lies, not really. She could read angles and lines, could size someone up and know they were the perfect suspect, but she couldn't distinguish promises from lies that were meant to be broken. What she could count were seconds, and she had spent too many of them here, in a place where Paul Hastie wasn't.

She snatched the notebook back from the receptionist and strode out the door, reading the address as she went. It wasn't far away, which was a blessing. But on the other hand, there was no telling how long he had been there, how much time he had had. He was already escalating his behavior, killing quicker, making bolder attacks. He could be claiming another victim even as she got back into the car and slammed the door shut, starting the engine and pulling out while simultaneously tugging the seatbelt over her body.

As she drove, she considered the possibility of calling for backup. The local PD would be quick on the scene, even if the sheriff was too far away. This was out of his zone. Backup would be the sensible choice. Safety in numbers, someone to make sure that he could not escape, to subdue him without bloodshed. Calculations flashed through her head. How far away they were from the precinct, how quickly a car could drive to the scene, how many men she should ask for.

But more people on the scene would mean more witnesses. Witnesses that could testify as to her behavior. She didn't want witnesses. She wanted Paul Hastie to run, to try and get away from her across empty land or into an abandoned building, somewhere where no one else could see them. She wanted to catch him alone. She wanted to hurt him. To make him pay for what he had done to Shelley.

Zoe tightened her hands on the steering wheel and pressed down the accelerator. She didn't reach for her cell phone to make the call. She would do this on her own.

Zoe slowed the car to a normal pace as she entered the road she wanted, trying to pass for a normal driver. The speedometer ticked down rapidly through numbers, until she saw something that looked somewhat legal. It wouldn't do to attract attention now. If he saw a car come screeching up to the house, he might get away or put a knife to someone's throat and cause a situation. She needed stealth.

She crept along the road as she slowed to a crawl, comparing house numbers to the address she was looking for. There was always a pleasing regularity to house numbers, the way they could be predicted to flow up one block and down the next. Easy to follow. She counted them off into the distance, identifying the correct home. Her head carried on without her, counting off into the distance over the next fifteen houses, almost distracting her enough that she didn't react in time. She pulled the car to a stop on the sidewalk next to the house, putting it into park and peering at the building.

The front door opened, and Zoe instinctively ducked, putting herself out of view. A moment later she sat up and pulled down the sun visor, pretending to look into the mirror on the back of it as an excuse to shield her face with it. Through the small gap between the visor and the edge of the window she watched them. Her window was already rolled down, allowing the sound of their conversation to drift across the way.

"Thanks, Paul, we really appreciate it," one of them was saying. A man in his fifties, balding and graying on top. He wore a comfortable flannel shirt and slacks one size too large. The homeowner. He was five foot seven. He weighed a hundred and fifty pounds. None of this mattered.

In a gray suit that matched precisely the shade Zoe had seen on the two employees at his office, the other man reached out to shake the homeowner's hand. Employee number three. No. He was six feet tall. He weighed one hundred seventy-five. He was exactly the right shape and size. "Don't mention it, Barry. We're going to get you all of the information you need to file your claim within the next five working days, all right? I don't want you to be left without for too long."

"That's perfect," Barry said, shaking the hand with a smile. Three pumps up and down. "Honestly, you've really put our minds at ease. We didn't know what to expect."

"Hey, I'm human, same as you," Paul said. Zoe struggled to focus on his face, to stop calculating the dimensions of it, to see what he actually *looked* like. "I know how distressing it can be when something's happened that wasn't your fault, and you're facing a huge bill. Those emergencies always seem to crop up when we can least afford them, right?"

"That's right," Barry laughed.

"All right. I'll be in touch. Best of luck with that contractor."

Zoe felt frozen, watching and listening to the exchange. She hadn't had the time to pull up anything on Paul Hastie himself, to see what he looked like. He was handsome, charismatic. Smiling an all-American white-toothed smile as he waved a final time to the homeowner, who was clearly impressed with him. He sounded . . . nice. Like a nice guy.

He was the furthest thing she could have imagined from a sadistic, depraved serial killer going around casually beheading young women who vaguely resembled his ex-wife.

What if she was wrong?

Could she possibly have gone off on a tangent that wasn't supported by evidence? Confirmation bias was enough of a phenomenon that she couldn't say with confidence it would never happen to her. She'd done it in the past—only seeing the dots that connected the way she wanted them to, ignoring the outliers.

Did they even all really look like Michelle Hastie? Or was this just a symptom of her skill—seeing calculations and angles, making comparisons between faces where other people saw actual features? Features that, without the mathematics, looked completely different to the human eye?

He was beginning to reach the end of the lawn, and then he would be past her. He would hit the sidewalk in two steps and head to his car in fifteen and be gone. Zoe couldn't allow that to happen, even if she was wrong. Even if she had made a huge mistake in even coming here. She got out of the car, catching his attention as she did so.

Maybe it was something in her eyes. He stopped dead when he looked up and caught sight of her, his expression faltering. He looked—scared. He was slowly raising his hands in an instinctive gesture, holding them in front of him, a motion of appeasement. His black hair was neatly parted on top of his head at the exact level of the corner of his left eye. He looked professional. Smart. Not like a deranged psychopath at all.

"Oh my god," the homeowner called out from the doorway of his house. He stepped back, started fumbling inside the door. "Stay back. I'm calling the police!"

Zoe glanced at him, not comprehending. Why would he be so afraid? Both of them had reacted so strongly to her, as if she was the one with the penchant for chopping off heads with a bloody machete and not—oh. She looked down and saw the gun in her hands. She hadn't even realized she had pulled it out. It was pointed at Paul Hastie, pointed squarely at his chest, short enough of a distance away that her aim would be absolute and true.

The homeowner was gone, disappeared inside the house. Distantly, Zoe could hear him shouting. She tuned it out. It was only her and Paul now, standing in the bright sun in front of the house. A ray of light flashed off the metallic surface of her gun, shooting a beam into Paul's eyes and making him wince. He lifted his hands higher, warding off the effect. Zoe saw the angle with detached observation, noting that when she tilted the gun a slightly different way the beam hit the ground instead.

Zoe couldn't think straight. Either Paul Hastie was the killer or he wasn't, and there was no getting around that. It was an absolute: black and white. She just couldn't figure out which side he fell down on. He didn't look how she would have expected. Even now. He wasn't murderous. He was scared. His eyes pleaded with her not to shoot him. To let him go. He didn't even say a word, his mouth hanging open in shock and fear.

Zoe groped in the darkness for instruction. What was she supposed to do? Where was Shelley, to be her moral compass, her people reader? To tell her whether this was their man or not?

There was only one thing she could think of. One thing that might give her a reaction she could read. She opened her mouth and the words tumbled out, helplessly, an accusation or a question.

"Michelle Griffiths," she said, using the woman's maiden name, because she wanted him to know that she had connected the dots—if there were truly dots to connect.

A change came over Paul Hastie's face. The fear began to slip, like paint dripping away. It ran like melting plastic until the mask was gone completely, and she saw something else underneath. Something in his eyes that chilled her to the bone. He was furious. Furious and self-mocking, because he knew that he had been caught.

He kept the eye contact for a single moment, and then ran.

CHAPTER TWENTY SEVEN

Zoe took off after him, the split-second delay it took her to react a curse. She re-aimed the gun and fired, but he had ducked behind some bushes that ran along the side of the house, and she couldn't see him. She raced around the side of the hedge hoping to see blood on the ground, but there was none. Only his retreating figure, moving rapidly away from her toward an open backyard.

Zoe flung herself after him, shouldering aside a swinging wooden gate that he had thrown shut behind him. Out in the back of the house there was space, wide space—a deck closer to the home and then open expanse before a three-foot fence, which he was already vaulting.

He was too far ahead, and Zoe needed to run too fast to be able to line up a shot. She saved her breath instead of yelling the curse that she wanted to and raced after him, gripping the wooden fence with her free hand to propel herself over it just as he had done. He was moving right ahead across an empty expanse of unused land, zigzagging like a rabbit, already moving up to the crest of a low hill.

Zoe followed his footsteps, knowing that she couldn't just follow him for long. She would need to find an advantage somewhere. If she didn't, he would stay ahead until she ran out of steam. She could see it in the athletic lines of his body. Even in the suit, he had the physique of a runner. He was practiced. This was his home terrain. She hadn't been anywhere near here in fifteen years.

She crested the low hill just as he had, catching sight of him heading toward another low knoll. She took a snapshot of the surrounding area in her head as she carried on moving: a busy highway to the far left, crowded with vehicles moving at high speed. Ahead, the waste land spread onward toward what must have been another town in the distance. To the right, more residential streets.

Where would he go? To the highway—no. Too much danger there for a man on foot, too unusual for someone to be walking or running there at all, especially in a suit. Even if he lost her, he wouldn't blend in. There was no escape for him there.

To the town ahead? It was a long way. Easy for someone to cut him off before he reached it. No, he would go right—back into the town—try to blend in on some busy street or duck into a building.

Zoe couldn't let that happen. Once he got back into a residential area, one that he knew well and she was a stranger to, he would be gone. The local PD weren't here. It was only her.

She cut off at a tangent, heading directly towards the backyard fences that closed off the residential side of the land. He was only heading straight to confuse her. She knew he would wait until she was far enough behind and then cut away, hoping that she wouldn't see him because of the hilly terrain until he was gone. He would disappear into thin air.

Not on her watch.

The hills formed a pattern of obstacles that blocked her view, affording him a glimpse of her now and then. He, too, must have lost sight of her. She was no longer where he expected her to be. She hoped this would count enough in her favor to give her the advantage, that he wouldn't figure out her plan and change his own course. If he stayed in the right place—if he was where she thought he would be—she slowed just enough to get her gun raised again, to hold it out in front of her, to point it at a ninety-five-degree angle to her left—

And fire, just as he came into view past the next hillock, running away and at an angle from her.

Zoe's breath caught in her throat as he tripped and fell to the ground, then came up and rolled, gripping his leg with a groan of pain and frustration that carried easily.

She raced across the distance between them, still keeping the gun outstretched. She gained on him easily, and he was still lying on his back when she drew up, panting, beside him.

"Bitch," he spat, still cradling his lower leg. He looked at her with unbridled hatred, a snarling animal now with his fangs out, no more human mask.

"Paul Hastie," Zoe said, reaching for the cuffs hooked into the back of her belt. "I'm arresting you for . . ."

The words trailed off and died in the back of her throat. *The murder of Special Agent Shelley Rose.* She couldn't say them. Couldn't give them life.

She looked at him. Really looked at him. This creature rocking and gasping on the ground, blood streaming from a shallow wound on the side of his leg where she had managed to clip him, a slash right through the gray material of his tailored pants. He wasn't handsome anymore. He was vicious, all teeth and claws, and he would rather bite her head off than be captured here and now.

Zoe let her hand drop away from the cuffs. She changed the angle of the gun in her hand, spinning it so that the hard surface of the handle was pointing toward him, clipping the safety back on. She paused just a moment longer.

And fell on him, dropping down with her knees on either side of him, knocking his arms away from his leg and pinning them to his sides. The butt of the gun came down against his nose and she felt and heard it shatter, the bone splintering away at the wrong angle, ruining the perfect aquiline line down from his brow.

And she brought it down again. Everything was lines and trajectories: down here at this angle with this much force, break the line of the jawbone. Turn his head with your fingers, grip his chin while he tries to roar with pain and finds he no longer can. Now here, at this speed down upon the line of the bone on the other side, a shallower angle because it is closer to you, feel it smash and dislocate. Another line, the cheekbone. Take every line you can see and smash it, break it, disrupt it. Destroy the pattern. Make his mask unusable. Everything else faded away, just Zoe with her angles and numbers, patterns and trajectories, pure and easy, white-hot, the only thing in the world.

Something was pulling at her arms and at first she resisted, stubbornly swinging the gun downward one more time to target the next unbroken line, but the pull was harder and then she was stumbling backward. Someone was barking her name, her rank, into her ear.

Zoe looked up and recognized the captain from the local precinct, turned her head and saw that one of them holding her back was Sergeant Daison. He was watching her with some level of horror, gazing at her face and the arm he was holding back—her arm—covered in blood, splashed all the way across her fist and the butt of her gun...

Zoe looked back down, at Paul Hastie and what she had made of him. His face was a mess. It was bloodied everywhere, splattered with spray and coated with gushes that even now still surged forward, his eyes and cheeks and jaw already beginning to swell and puff. He was making a thin gurgling noise, the blood in his nose and mouth bubbling as he breathed. He lay still as the officers milled around him, no longer trying to get up and run. His eyes, almost hidden already by the blood and the swelling, were fixed on her. She tried to count the number of bones she had broken in his face and lost track of the number.

"Agent Prime." Daison gaped. "You'd better come back to the precinct with us."

CHAPTER TWENTY EIGHT

Zoe stared straight ahead at the wall of the interrogation room. It was both strange and comforting that the inside of these things almost always looked the same, or at least a variation on one of two themes. Either a single dank room with a table and chairs, in plain colors with no decoration; or the same, but with the addition of black glass, possible to see into the room but not out of it.

This was of the simpler breed. She wasn't being watched. It was just as well; she had switched off everything since she had been put in here, all of the attempts to control her face, to blend in, to have any kind of expression. She was blank, staring straight ahead at the empty wall, because that was the safest place to look. Smooth, featureless from ceiling to floor. Nothing to count, though she could measure it, calculate angles and trajectories. At least that was less of a distraction than normal.

The mist of rage that had covered her eyes had gradually faded away, leaving her back inside herself, aware and awake. She had only scattered memories of what had happened after she caught up with Paul Hastie. The chase was clear to her, but after that it all went hazy, like a movie you'd watched as a child where you could no longer remember the ending or the plot.

The door rattled momentarily, the only warning that it was about to open, and then Sergeant Daison poked his head into the room. "Agent Prime," he said, breaking her silent concentration. "I thought you'd like to know. We found a leather blackjack and machete in his apartment. Both had been cleaned, but forensics think there's a good chance of getting some trace DNA samples from small areas that were missed. It should be enough to put him away."

"Thank you." Zoe said. She felt like she was coming out of a deep sleep—her muscles stiff and aching, her brain coming to terms with reality. "What about the medical report?"

Daison made a shrug and twisted his face in a way that Zoe couldn't interpret. "He'll live. You broke a fair few bones, but he'll live. With the addition of a pin or two."

Zoe couldn't say she felt sorry. She had no connection, now, to the blind fury that had come over her—it felt like it had come from someone else. She didn't regret it, either. It just was.

"I, um." Daison hesitated. He glanced behind him and then slipped fully through the door, letting it shut behind him temporarily. "I don't know if I'm supposed to tell you this, but they found his ex-wife's head. Michelle Hastie. It was in a freezer in his garage."

"What about the other heads?" Zoe asked. *All except Shelley*, she didn't add out loud, because Shelley's had been the only one left for her to find.

"Nothing yet. I expect we'll find them sooner or later. He's probably got them stashed somewhere else."

Zoe nodded. What else was there to say?

"They're going to charge him with all of them," Daison added, reopening the door and starting to back out of it. "They've got enough, thanks to the weapons and the regularity of his MO."

Zoe knew that the information was intended to reassure her, to promise her that her partner would see justice in court along with the rest of them. She could only nod to that, too. It was something. And it was nothing. It wouldn't bring Shelley back.

Daison gave her a nod in return and slipped away, out into the gentle noise of the corridor and back to real life. Zoe sighed, stirring in her chair. It was probably approaching time that she returned to real life, too.

She looked down at her own hands. Her knuckles were crusted with blood, both Hastie's and her own. She needed to get herself cleaned up before anything else. She stood, flexing her hands into fists. The cuts across her knuckles cracked open again, issuing a thin stream of new, bright red blood across the old crimson.

She was suddenly loath to touch the door handle with her dirty hands, but it wasn't as though she was getting out of here any other way. She pushed her way outside and began down the corridor, seeking the cool tiles and silence of the women's bathroom. She made it there without any more enforced social interactions and stared at herself in the mirror. There were a few flecks of blood on her face where it had sprayed up from her fists as she hit him. She doused her whole face in cold water, letting it drip over her collar and slick down the hair over her ears. She looked like she was half-mad. Maybe she was.

Having dried herself off with paper towels and managed to stanch the bleeding from her knuckles again, Zoe gave herself one last glance in the mirror and took a breath. She attempted to put some kind of normal, friendly expression on her face and saw only a pale imitation of what it should be, so she dropped it.

She headed out into the corridor, intending to find the captain and take her leave. As she passed down the hall, two officers appeared coming from the reception area, leading a woman between them. Paul Hastie's girlfriend, Zoe realized, catching sight of her doll-like face and petite figure. What was her name again? Victoria?

She was trembling even as she walked, her face wet with tears and streaked with red. She glanced up as Zoe passed by, then turned away, fresh liquid pooling in her eyes. Zoe stopped and watched as they led her into an interrogation room, then left her, closing the door behind them.

"That's Victoria Lee," she said. It was a statement rather than a question, but still intended as something of a conversation starter.

"The captain wanted her in for questioning," one of the officers explained. He didn't ask who she was. Zoe figured they probably all knew by now. The mad FBI agent who had gone nuclear on the suspect. "Poor thing. She's badly shaken up. When we told her what her boyfriend had done she wouldn't stop crying. Never suspected a thing."

Zoe twitched an eyebrow. "She suspected something. I went to see her, not long ago. Told her to stay away from him to save her life. She knew why I was looking for him."

"It's another thing to know it for sure, though, isn't it?" the other officer said sympathetically. "Being suspected of something is a lot different than us finding a head in his fridge. Now she knows it's true. She was dating a killer. Doesn't bear thinking about, them snuggled up and whispering sweet nothings after he'd gone and beheaded some young woman."

"It was in his freezer," Zoe corrected him absent-mindedly, turning away. There was something here that was catching on her attention, though she couldn't figure out what. Something that didn't quite add up.

She trailed through toward the captain's office, thinking. She halted outside the main doors to the bullpen, remembering that she would have to cross a sea of people in order to get to him. The idea filled her with dread. She hesitated, and the doors opened to emit a waft of loud noise and activity, officers and suspects bustling about together, almost overwhelming her senses.

"Agent Prime?"

The doors shut behind him, and Zoe took a breath before looking up and recognizing that it was Captain Tarroway himself who had emerged. That was luck. She found herself wishing it was Sheriff Hawthorne whose jurisdiction they had ended up in, not this stranger. At least Hawthorne knew her, knew Shelley. It would have been more comfortable by far.

"I am heading out," Zoe said. "Thought it best to let you know."

"Thanks for letting me know," the captain said. He was looking away from her, down the corridor. "I guess you'll have your own briefings and so on to attend to. We're fine taking it from here."

He was striding away. Zoe couldn't tell if he was eager to finish the job and get the questioning done, or if he was eager to get away from her. She hadn't exactly covered herself in glory when she took Hastie down. There were spots of blood on the cuffs of her shirt. She tugged down the sleeve of her jacket, realizing that it, too, was stiff with the stuff. It was dark enough that the color only showed if you looked closely.

She felt a shiver run over her body: time to get changed. She didn't want to be clothed in the blood of a murderer—anyone's blood, but his most of all—for too much longer. But even so, she hesitated as she passed by the interrogation room where she had seen Victoria Lee enter.

What was it, that thing nagging at the back of her mind? It was that itching sensation that came when something didn't quite add up.

It came to her in the form of a question, a question that she needed to have answered. It wouldn't wait. Something in her gut was calling to her, telling her that now was the time. Zoe rushed at the door, pushing it open and barging into in the middle of the interview, catching three shocked faces looking back at her: Daison, Tarroway, and Victoria Lee herself.

"Agent Prime," Tarroway began, his voice reproachful. "We're conducting an interview here—"

"So am I," Zoe said.

Tarroway started to get to his feet, his chair scraping back with a metallic sound. He and Daison both wore worried expressions. Maybe they thought she was about to go psycho on Victoria, just like she had done with Hastie. But this wasn't like that. She was in control.

"I'm going to have to ask you to leave, Agent, this isn't ..."

Zoe held up a hand, cutting him off again. He was moving toward her, arms spread, intending to shepherd her back out of the door. She wouldn't let that happen. She couldn't. There was no time to reason with him—no way she could risk missing her window of opportunity. She had to get to the bottom of this, to ask the question that had come to her mind.

"Victoria," she said, raising her voice so that she could be heard, moving onto her tiptoes and craning her head to keep sight of Hastie's girlfriend. "What were you doing at home in the middle of the day?"

"What?" Victoria replied, gasping slightly, her face still puffy and wet. Even Tarroway hesitated, surprised at the question.

"Earlier today I came to see you unannounced, and you were at home, waiting. Why were you not out at work?"

"Well, I—I don't have a job at the moment," Victoria stuttered. "I haven't been working for the last month."

Tarroway had halted his advance, his arms drooping toward his sides slightly. He was keeping Zoe in his line of sight but tilting his head back to one side, assessing Victoria's reactions as well. His resolve to throw her out had obviously faltered. Zoe pressed home the advantage. There was something here, some buried bone. She just had to keep digging to get to it.

"Where were you working before this month?"

"I was a receptionist," Victoria said. She was looking between Daison and Tarroway hurriedly, as if expecting them to help her out, to give some kind of explanation for this line of questioning.

"For who?" Zoe demanded.

"A doctor." Victoria hesitated. Zoe had often found that simply not replying to someone at all, watching them, was the best way to convince them to fill the awkward silence with more information. "Dr. Edgerton. He was suspended recently—there's talk of a lawsuit against him, so I'm out of work. They haven't hired anyone to replace him yet. Why is this relevant?"

Like the final piece of a jigsaw puzzle fitting into place, everything clicked for Zoe. She saw it now. The whole picture.

"You are very good, Victoria," Zoe said quietly. She was resting in a relaxed posture now, Tarroway no longer trying to herd her away. She reached behind her to close the door, shutting them all in. "You agree, do you not? You play it very convincingly."

Victoria blinked. Something passed behind her eyes for a moment—a fragment of a moment—the tiniest thing, so quick that even Zoe would not have been sure she had seen it if she wasn't deliberately looking for it. Then the façade of confused innocence resumed, and Victoria even managed to be tearful when she replied. "Play what? What's going on?"

"Agent Prime?" Captain Tarroway said. It was clear what he really wanted to say: what *was* going on? He didn't appreciate being kept in the dark in the middle of an interrogation.

But Zoe didn't have the headspace to care about him or whether he would be put out by being the last to know. She had it now—all of it. All of the pieces, lined up so neatly. It was like a model of the solar system in her head. Paul Hastie, circling the image of his dead wife like she was the sun, picking off any other woman who entered his orbit. Behind him, like a moon shadowing its planet, Victoria Lee. A trigger, dictating the pull of the tides, dominating the darkness.

She wasn't an innocent girlfriend just learning for the first time that her partner was a killer. The doe-eyed innocence, the tears, all of it was just an act. She was as much a part of this as Hastie was.

"You helped him find them," Zoe said. It wasn't a question. It was a statement of truth. "You knew the women from the patient lists. You knew it would be easy to make it look like Dr. Edgerton was involved somehow. You did it so well we even arrested him. We were going to make him take the blame for all of it, until Paul got ahead of himself and decided to take my partner out. You thought that you were going to get away with all of it—is that not true?"

Victoria blinked at her slowly. There was a red flush on her cheeks, but the tears were gone. Somewhere inside there, she was steady. Wearing a mask. Playing the innocent. "I-I don't know what you mean, what you're talking about. Officers, please, what is she . . .?"

"You chose them because they would remind Paul of Michelle," Zoe said. "You wanted to make sure that he would not falter. You knew he was a killer—when you got together, maybe, or soon after, you found out. Maybe it was even you who encouraged him to kill Michelle in the first place. You were jealous that he had someone before you. Am I getting close?"

In a way, it was a genuine question. Zoe could guess. But the only way she was going to unravel it all for sure would be through a confession. She just had to play it like Shelley would have. Use psychology. Emotions. Get inside Victoria Lee's head until she blurted it out by accident, or because she thought she could trust Zoe.

But it wasn't working—not yet.

"I don't know what you're talking about," Victoria said again, her breath catching on a tearful hitch. She looked at Tarroway, clearly seeing him as the most sympathetic face in the room. "Please, this is—I've cooperated fully. I've told you everything. I had no idea about Paul. I feel sick about it. Please, I don't know what she's saying."

Tarroway started to rise to his feet, force of habit driving his hands to button up his jacket. "Agent Prime, I think that's enough for now. We've got this under control."

"No, you have not," Zoe snapped. She felt the anger flooding back into her, the rage. This woman was responsible. She had picked out Shelley. Told Paul Hastie to cut her head off. She wasn't going to get away with it.

Tarroway looked at her in alarm, raising his hands in front of him. "Now, Agent Prime. Let's just step outside, shall we?"

Zoe knew he was scared she was about to lose her temper again. To go at Victoria Lee the way she had gone at Paul Hastie. But she wasn't. She was in control now. The rage inside of her was burning cold, not hot. In a way, maybe that should have scared him more. But she warded off his corralling arms, stepping to the side, behind the table, away from the door.

"Captain Tarroway, I outrank you here," she said. It wasn't pretty, but when all you had in your favor was rank, you had to use it.

She had to push. Had to keep pushing. Victoria had already resorted to begging the other officers with tears in her eyes to save her from the big, bad FBI agent. That must mean she was close to cracking. It was a defense mechanism, crocodile tears to proclaim her innocence. Zoe knew, the way she knew the sun was going to come up in the morning and wild dogs weren't to be petted, what Shelley would have done. She felt it in her gut. She had to push, and keep pushing until Victoria Lee broke.

"I think you were together before Michelle Hastie died," Zoe said. She ignored Tarroway completely, only feeling a narrow flare of victory when he dropped his arms and slowly sat back in his chair, keeping his eyes on her. "Is that true, Victoria? Tell me. We can easily find out."

"Yes," Victoria said, reluctantly. Her eyes were red-rimmed, but they were no longer dripping tears. She had switched gears already. "We were together a little while before."

Zoe nodded. She stayed where she was, a few paces behind and between the two policemen, dominating the room. Holding a position of power. "That is what I thought." She pressed her hand to her chin as if thinking, the other arm folded across her body. "I can see how it all worked, Victoria. After you got together, you started to encourage him. You started to tell him that it would be so easy to get Michelle out of the way. To end her life forever. To stop the alimony payments, to stop her from interfering in your lives. You told Paul that would be the answer to all his problems, and you would help. You would not leave him."

"No," Victoria said, though her voice was faltering.

"Yes. You saw that in him, saw he could be a killer. That was what attracted you to him in the first place. The coldness inside him, the disconnect from what normal people think and feel. You saw he had that potential. It was what broke up his marriage, and you saw that you could use it. You could make him into a weapon."

"This doesn't make any sense," Victoria muttered, her voice small and girlish, an obvious appeal to the men in the room.

"It makes sense to you. You had this desire, deep down inside of you, is that not right? You saw in him what you saw in yourself. That same lack of feeling. And what you wanted, what you wanted more than anything, was to sow destruction and chaos. To take lives."

"I would never..." Victoria protested, her voice trailing off. She was still engaged, arguing with Zoe every step of the way. That was good. It meant that she felt she needed to argue her case. She saw Zoe as a threat, not a joke. She was worried.

"You worked on Paul for weeks, I bet," Zoe continued, her arms folded across her chest together now. "Told him about men who had got away with killing their wives. Maybe you talked to him about machetes, about methods of execution. About the way revenge killings are carried out. You talked and talked until he started to think that maybe killing his wife would be a viable option. And then you helped him to make plans, real plans, and to carry them out."

"She was his ex-wife," Victoria said. It seemed like she couldn't help herself. She was shaking her head, too, but the outburst had come from deep inside of her. She couldn't hold it back. She was cracking, slowly. Zoe couldn't stop now.

"You got a thrill out of it, right? Controlling him. Having him kill people for you, like a weapon you could aim and fire. Wiping people out without having to get your own hands dirty. Just like playing God. Picking out someone whose face you did not like, someone who would appeal to Paul, and then sending him off to kill them. Waiting in the car for him to drop into the passenger seat with a severed head and a bloody machete, to show you the terror in their eyes before he ended them."

Victoria said nothing. She was still shaking her head mutely, staring at the table, unable to look up at Zoe. She was close now. Zoe could feel it, could see her mask slipping in real time. Just a little further—

"I bet it was all so easy for you. Saying just the right things in his ear, putting on displays for him. Pretending to be upset or hurt so that he would take them for you. Pretending that you loved him so he would stay loyal. Abusing his trust. Controlling him."

"I do love him!" Victoria burst out. Her eyes had snapped up to Zoe, and there was something new blazing inside them now: a kind of righteous anger, as if she had been doing the right thing all along and couldn't bear to be challenged on it. "I always loved him! It was her who didn't—his ex—*she* was the abusive one, the controlling one. He had to get rid of her. She was always going to have a hold over him if he didn't, and he was never going to be able to love me back fully while she still had her claws in him, making him sleep with her whenever she wanted! She deserved to die!"

"She deserved to die." Zoe repeated it slowly, flatly. For all the anger that Victoria radiated out, Zoe reflected back none of it, blank and emotionless. "But what about the others you made him kill?"

"Stupid bitches," Victoria twisted her face, her features transforming from a beautiful little doll to something grotesque and unrecognizable. "He was always tempted by girls that reminded him of her. I couldn't let him be tempted. They had to go."

Zoe had been angling herself forward, leaning closer and closer over the policemen's heads toward Victoria. She straightened now, taking a few steps back. "Thank you, Victoria," she said, without any real warmth behind the words. "Captain Tarroway, I will let you do the honors."

She glanced down for the first time in a while and saw both Daison and Tarroway looking around at her with stunned expressions. They didn't seem to know what to say. Tarroway gathered himself with a visible effort and turned back around to face Victoria, clearing his throat.

"Victoria Lee," he said. "I am arresting you as an accomplice to murder. You have the right to remain silent and refuse to answer questions..."

Zoe stopped paying attention to him, his voice fading off as she watched Victoria Lee. She watched the girl's face. She went from defiant anger to a kind of delayed shock and realization, then guilt at the knowledge she had effectively confessed, then impotent anger again. The tears gathering in her eyes this time were real. They were the eyes of someone realizing they had just put themselves behind bars for the rest of their life.

Zoe had seen and heard enough. She was no longer needed here. She swept toward the door and out of the room, slamming it shut behind her so Victoria Lee could hear what it was like to be caged, a little taste of what was to come. Then she strode out of the precinct and hailed the first cab she saw to take her to the airport.

Epilogue

Zoe straightened the lapels of the black suit jacket she was wearing for perhaps the fifteenth time. She couldn't say exactly why, but somehow it mattered that she was neat and tidy today. The way that Shelley had always been: so put together, even when she was called into a case on a moment's notice in the middle of the night. If it was the one thing that Zoe could do to honor her, then she had to do it.

She stood apart from the rest of the group, watching. It was an old cliché, but what was she supposed to do? Go over there and stand shoulder to shoulder with Shelley's family? Look her husband in the face? Squeeze her infant daughter's hand?

No. She stayed under the shade of an ash tree, one hand on the bark for support. From here, she could just about hear the minister reading the service. The grave yawned wide at his feet, like an opening direct into the maw of hell. Zoe couldn't bring herself to look at it. She focused on him instead, the way he read aloud with the Bible open in his hands, even though he clearly knew the words by heart.

She had long let her eyes go soft, letting go of the focus. If she didn't focus, then it was only a mass of black shapes around the grave: formless beings, who had neither face nor personality. They could have been anyone. The added benefit was that if she didn't look at them, she wouldn't have to count them, to know their respective heights and weights and ages, to compare statistics on hats versus veils, suits versus dresses.

Not that it helped much. The slow and even cadence of the man's voice that floated across the distance to her was lulling, giving her little to focus on. She was aware of the sixty-three gravestones scattered across the field behind him. The pattern of the trees, indicating a natural growth but the unnatural removal

173

of their brothers in order to space them out and leave room for the bodies. The sun gleaming off the roof of a car in the parking lot bright enough to blind her, casting a shadow that told her it was around 11:30 a.m., shining over a half-inch deep puddle that had formed in a dip in the tarmac.

It had rained all night, ceaseless and relentless. Zoe had been glad. She'd thought that she could stand here and watch the service and the rain would fall down her cheeks like tears, and she wouldn't have to pretend that she had any left to give because no one would be able to tell the difference. But instead, an hour before the service was due to begin, the sun had broken through the clouds. Now everything shimmered with a dewy brightness, an impression of new life, and Zoe hid her stone-carved face in the shadow of a tree.

The service was coming to a close. Zoe watched as Harry and little Amelia threw, together, a pair of white roses down into the void below them, and had to fight hard to remember how to breathe again.

She should turn and go, she thought, leave this place behind. It was over now. But she couldn't quite think of where to go. Her cell phone was buzzing in her pocket again, the way it had all morning. Zoe looked at the display for lack of anything else to do and saw that it was Dr. Applewhite calling, and put the device back into her pocket. Eventually, the buzzing stopped.

She thought about her empty flat, about the open road, about work. Nothing seemed to fit. She would have turned and fled, but the mourners seemed to be heading in the opposite direction to where she stood. The more they moved away, the more she could see of the grave itself, the waiting pile of dirt. She thought about spending eternity under that weight, pressing down on the top of an airless coffin.

"Zoe?"

The voice was a surprise, but Zoe didn't jump. She slowly looked up, having difficulty refocusing her eyes to take in Special Agent in Charge Leo Maitland, standing there beside her in formal uniform with his cap under his arm. Where had he come from? She had been so focused on the grave she hadn't even seen.

"Zoe," he said again, now that she was looking at him. "I'm sorry."

Zoe nodded mechanically. Everyone was sorry for her loss. Even though it wasn't entirely hers. Harry and Amelia, that was who they should be sorry for.

"I've been trying to get in contact with you," Maitland said. His voice was a deep rumble, like thunder across the sky. Appropriate, given the morning's weather. "You didn't come back in for your debriefing when you returned home."

Zoe stirred slightly. Of course. There were still things that had to be done, things to take care of. Procedure and routine. There was some small comfort in that.

"I will come in tomorrow," she said. Today was too much. Besides, Maitland himself was here. There would be no one to lead the debrief.

"No." Maitland seemed to be having trouble meeting her eyes, looking at some interesting spot a foot and a half away on the ground. "Actually, it's good that you haven't come in. I'm ... I'm sorry to do this here and now, of all places, but I don't have a lot of choice. If you'd come in ..."

Zoe waited patiently, watching him. He seemed to feel awkward about something, though she didn't know what. It was as if he wanted her to finish his sentence, but she had no idea how it ended.

"Agent Prime, I have to put you on temporary suspension," Maitland said. "After your act of brutality towards Paul Hastie, you've been placed under investigation by internal affairs. You won't return to active duty unless your conduct is cleared."

"Oh," she said. "I see."

She turned from the tree and walked back to her car, not giving him a backwards glance even when he called her name.

Zoe closed the door behind her and sank down into the armchair in her living room without bothering to take off her boots. Pythagoras and Euler, her cats, mewed at her for a few moments. They were used to her preparing food for them when she came in, but it was the middle of the day.

Euler sniffed around at her feet for a moment, then stretched his elegant back and jumped up onto the arm of the chair. A swift prowling motion carried him up and behind her, walking along the raised back, until he settled into a comfortable position. His tail hung down next to her face, close enough to touch but still distant. Even the cats sensed the emptiness in her.

Zoe sat in silence, staring out at the far side of the room, at the dark and empty television set. She didn't move, not even to pet the cats. Pythagoras stalked away in search of something more interesting. Outside, the light gradually began to fade, the sun moving until it ducked behind another apartment building that blocked half of her window, leaving one part of the room in darkness and another in bright brilliance.

The cell phone in her pocket rang again, startling Zoe enough that she dug it out of her pocket without thinking. She looked at the display and hesitated. It wasn't Dr. Applewhite again. It was John, his smiling face coming up on the screen, a reminder of a time that felt like it must have been impossibly long ago.

She hadn't spoken to him since that last call. They had made plans, and she had never bothered to follow through. He had called her since, several times, sent messages. All of them pleading with her to talk to him, to tell her if he had done something wrong. He hadn't done anything. He deserved at least to not have to keep calling.

Zoe answered the call as Euler hopped down to the floor with a yowl of disapproval at the loud noise, and put it onto speakerphone. She rested the device on her knee so she wouldn't have to hold it up. Her arms felt tired. Too tired to lift it.

"John."

"Zoe! Jesus Christ, I've been trying to get ahold of you. Did you see my messages?"

"Yes." Zoe couldn't give him more than that. Didn't bother to explain. She didn't have the words inside her to offer him.

There was a brief pause. John had probably expected her to give an explanation. Maybe he was taken aback by the directness of it. Maybe he'd thought her phone was broken or lost, or she had been in a coma in a ditch somewhere, incapable of answering. Zoe counted the seconds, one, two, three—

"Well, what happened?" John asked. His voice was muted now, a note of sympathy creeping in. Poor John. He couldn't imagine that Zoe would ignore him without a good reason.

Maybe he hadn't seen the news, or maybe the story hadn't even broken this far down the country. The death of an FBI agent wasn't entirely unusual. Law enforcement officials died all the time. In Nebraska it was probably big news, but maybe not here.

Zoe opened her mouth, then closed it again. She couldn't say it. Couldn't tell him what had happened. She couldn't say Shelley's name. He was going to end up hating her, but that was fine. That was expected. What else could she do?

"John," she said, her voice strangely flat and toneless even to her own ears. "I do not want to see you anymore."

"What?" There was a pause, then John continued, more animated, his voice rising in volume and pitch. "Zoe, has something happened? You don't sound right. You can talk to me."

"John," Zoe said again, sliding her eyes closed. "I do not want to see you anymore."

"But...why not?" John sounded desperate now, like a wounded animal crying in the woods. Zoe thought with detachment that it was not an altogether attractive side of him. "Things were going well. Really well, I thought. Zoe, we can meet up and talk about this—"

"No." Zoe couldn't give him a single shred of hope. Couldn't leave him with that. It wasn't fair. There wasn't any hope for them, none at all. He had to know that, or it would be too cruel. "Please do not call me again. I do not want to talk about it. I do not want to see you."

"Just like that?" John sounded like he was getting the point now, though he still wanted to argue. "But, Zoe, we..."

"Goodbye, John." Zoe reached out and touched the red icon on her screen, ending the call.

Silence settled over the room again. She left the cell phone where it sat, her arm falling down onto the seat of the armchair beside her leg. Even Euler and Pythagoras were gone, out in some other room, avoiding her. They knew the truth.

It wasn't just John. Zoe wouldn't be seeing anyone. Not now and not in the future. She didn't deserve them. Didn't deserve his goodness, his patience, his affection. She was as she had always been: a loner, a stranger. She had known since she was a child that she was different, apart. Forgetting that, pretending that she could have something more, had been a mistake.

It wasn't one that she was going to make again.

Zoe sat in silence and watched the sun go down over the city outside her window, until the room was dark, and she still didn't move at all.

Now Available for Pre-Order!

FACE OF FURY
(A Zoe Prime Mystery—Book 5)

"A MASTERPIECE OF THRILLER AND MYSTERY. Blake Pierce did a magnificent job developing characters with a psychological side so well described that we feel inside their minds, follow their fears and cheer for their success. Full of twists, this book will keep you awake until the turn of the last page."
—Books and Movie Reviews, Roberto Mattos (re Once Gone)

FACE OF FURY is book #5 in a new FBI thriller series by USA Today best-selling author Blake Pierce, whose #1 bestseller Once Gone (Book #1) (a free download) has received over 1,000 five star reviews.

FBI Special Agent Zoe Prime suffers from a rare condition which also gives her a unique talent: she views the world through a lens of numbers. The numbers torment her, make her unable to relate to people, and give her a failed romantic life. Yet they also allow her to see patterns that no other FBI agent can.

In FACE OF FURY, women are turning up dead, victims of a serial killer who carves a mysterious symbol on their bodies. The symbol holds some mathematical significance, and Zoe struggles to know if he is killing in the order of PI.

But when her theory falls apart, Zoe must second guess everything she thought she knew.

Has Zoe's talent met its match? And can she save the next victim in time?

An action-packed psychological suspense thriller with heart-pounding suspense, FACE OF FURY is book #5 in a riveting new series that will leave you turning pages late into the night.

FACE OF FURY
(A Zoe Prime Mystery—Book 5)

Made in the USA
Middletown, DE
14 November 2022

14994069R00116